"Do you have ☜ W9-AZF-105

"I'm single," Alicia said firmly. Then, lest he think she was angling for a date, she added, "And I intend to stay that way."

"Not exactly what I asked." His gaze narrowed. "But I agree with you. I intend to stay single, too."

"Oh?" A hunk like him staying single? In Churchill? Alicia almost laughed.

"I will never allow myself to go through losing someone I care for again." The absolute loss in Jack's voice killed her amusement. When he spoke again, his voice was more even. "If you had kids, you'd understand how they become the focus of your life. You'll do anything for them. Giselle is my world. Besides her, nothing else matters."

I do understand what you mean, Jack. I know exactly how you feel. I'd do anything to keep my son safe. But I don't know where he is, or how to find him.

"Sorry, guess I'm not very good company tonight," Jack muttered, turning away. The keep-away signs were clearly posted. Only natural, given he'd lost his wife.

Not that Alicia was interested in Jack…

Books by Lois Richer

Love Inspired

LOIS RICHER

began her travels the day she read her first book and realized that fiction provided an extraordinary adventure. Creating that adventure for others became her obsession. With millions of books in print, Lois continues to enjoy creating stories of joy and hope. She and her husband love to travel, which makes it easy to find the perfect setting for her next story. Lois would love to hear from you via www.loisricher.com or loisricher@yahoo.com, or on Facebook.

North Country Mom
Lois Richer

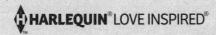

HARLEQUIN® LOVE INSPIRED®

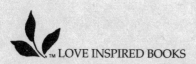

LOVE INSPIRED BOOKS

Recycling programs
for this product may
not exist in your area.

ISBN-13: 978-0-373-81764-1

NORTH COUNTRY MOM

Copyright © 2014 by Lois M. Richer

www.Harlequin.com

Printed in U.S.A.

The Lord will work out his plans for my life—
for your lovingkindness, Lord, continues forever.
Don't abandon me—for you made me.
—*Psalms* 138:8

This book is dedicated to my mom,
the strongest woman I know. I love you.

Chapter One

In her rush up the train stairs, Alicia Featherstone smacked headfirst into a massive male chest.

Her breath whooshed out and she reeled back, fighting to recover her balance.

"My fault." The man's voice reminded her of a polar bear's growl. His fingers closed around her arm, almost dragging her upward into the dim train.

His grasp sparked memories of the darkest moments in her life. Memories that threatened to engulf her.

"Please," Alicia gasped, fighting the remembered images while struggling to hold on to the three packages she cradled.

The shadows...his hands... She had to get free. But his strong grip wouldn't release her. She knew the stranger was trying to help, but years of nightmare memories of being attacked couldn't stem the panic clogging her throat.

The sound of her precious packages tumbling to the floor snapped her back to reality. One box bounced down the stairs and landed on the platform. She couldn't afford to lose it, certainly not because of this big man who'd blocked her way. With anger came clarity.

"Let go of me," she ordered.

His hand immediately dropped away. The man stepped back as if she'd burned him. Alicia inhaled, drawing in oxygen to ease the terror of the past.

"All aboard for Churchill, Manitoba!"

The conductor's call galvanized Alicia. She dropped what she held and hurried down the steps to retrieve her parcel from the platform. She'd barely gained the first step up when the train began moving. Again the man's massive hands closed over her arms. He hauled her upward until his face was millimeters from hers. His deep blue eyes blazed into hers.

"Jumping out like that was a stupid thing to do," he growled.

"Please—" she began, then clamped her mouth closed.

This isn't the past. You aren't fifteen and vulnerable. You don't have to beg.

"Release me," she demanded, then wished she hadn't. He was only trying to help; no point in antagonizing him. He might end up as a customer and

Alicia needed every buyer she could get to fulfill her dream of opening a second store.

"Sorry." He dropped her arm and held up his hands, backing away.

"Thank you. I'm going to find a seat," she said firmly as she bent to corral the rest of her packages. One box skittered beyond her reach.

"By all means." The man caught the runaway box and laid it on top of the others in her arms without touching her. Then he opened the heavy door, held it and waved her past.

"Thanks." Alicia tried to ignore his presence as she searched for a vacant seat.

It would have to be one of those days when the tired old train was full. Two of the most biased people in town were on board. Though it hurt, she pretended she didn't notice the way they turned their backs on her and hoped the man behind her didn't notice, either.

Finally she spied two seats together in the middle of the car. She hurried toward them, relieved to let her packages tumble onto the seat.

"Um." *He* was right behind her. "That's my seat."

"Oh." Her face reddened, but she wasn't going to be intimidated by either his height or his muscle-honed body. She twisted to look at him.

That was a mistake. His face nearly made her gulp. Classic hunk material. All chiseled lines and sharp-angled cheekbones topped by beach-bum-blond hair and rich blue eyes that seemed to bore into her. Alicia inhaled and focused.

"Both seats are yours?"

"Technically, one is my daughter's, but she's sleeping over there." He jerked a hand toward the seats across the aisle. A preteen girl lay sprawled across the two reclining chairs, her long black hair spread around her like a curtain. "Giselle wasn't feeling well earlier so I'd rather not wake her. It would be better if we could share these two seats." His short, terse tone dared her to argue. When she didn't respond, he glanced down at her packages spread across both seats then back up at her. "If you don't mind?"

Actually, Alicia did mind.

The intimacy of sitting beside him made her very uncomfortable. Besides, she'd counted on catching some sleep before the train arrived in Churchill tomorrow morning. With this heartthrob sitting next to her the chances of that were as good as her winning the lottery; however, as the last person to board the train she was hardly in a position to argue.

He tapped his toe, clearly impatient for her decision. As if she had a choice. Still…she was making progress in her whole *avoid men* issue. She could do this.

"Uh, thanks for sharing." Alicia tried to gather the packages, but she no sooner had a grip on two than the third popped out of her arms.

Usually she brought a bag for just this purpose, but somehow she'd misplaced it at the last stop when she'd left the train to pick up Mary Starblanket's beaded earrings. Frustrated and embarrassed that everyone was now watching them, she tried to hide below the seat back and in the process lost all the packages she held.

"Maybe this will help." He held out a sack made of netting. "I'll hold it, you get them inside. Perhaps then we can finally sit down."

"Thanks." So bossy. But at least he was helping. When the bag was full, he tightened the top then swung everything into an overhead bin, including her backpack. She winced at the rough handling but said only, "Window or aisle?"

"Aisle. My legs are too long for the inside seat."

They certainly were; long and clad in designer jeans. But it was his feet Alicia noticed—feet covered in a most amazing pair of boots which lovingly hugged his feet in gleaming black calfskin. For a fit like that, she guessed the boots were custom. She wondered who'd made them. Good craftsmen were hard to find. She should know. She was always looking for unique, handcrafted items for her shop.

Suddenly aware she was staring, Alicia huddled against the wall to give him more room.

His smile and the way he pointed his booted toes

up were the only signs he gave that he'd noticed her scrutiny. He thrust out a hand. "Jack Campbell."

"Alicia Featherstone." As his fingers engulfed hers a tiny shiver of—what? Fear? Dread?—made the hairs on her arm stand to attention. She blinked. No, it felt more like anticipation. Surprise bloomed inside her. It couldn't be anticipation. Men made her nervous. Had done ever since—

"What's in the packages, Alicia?" he asked.

"Stock for my store." He certainly wasn't reticent. "I buy handmade goods from First Nations people to sell to visitors to Churchill," she explained. "Canada has a thriving Native arts population. I'm trying to help it expand."

"Tansi."

This handsome traveler spoke her native Cree language? Delighted, Alicia shot back a greeting in the same language.

"Pardon?" Jack raised both eyebrows in an imperious question mark.

Uh-oh. Alicia switched to English. "I thought you were speaking to me in Cree."

"Maybe I was and didn't know it." His tanned face relaxed and suddenly he looked much younger. And more handsome, if that was possible. "I don't know what it means but isn't Tansi the name of your store?"

"In Cree it means 'hi' or 'how are you.'" She tilted

her head to one side. "And yes, my store is called Tansi. How did you know?"

"I've been to Churchill before." Jack inclined his head. "My sister, Laurel Quinn, lives there. She runs a rehabilitation project for troubled boys called Lives Under Construction."

"I'm very familiar with it. I teach her boys classes on Aboriginal culture." Alicia silently completed a second inventory on Jack. Yep, he was the stuff of romantic teenage dreams. Fortunately hers were long gone. "How long will you be visiting?"

She followed his gaze to the girl who slept so peacefully across the way. Giselle didn't look anything like her father. *Perhaps she favors her mother.* A pang of loss pinched Alicia's stomach into a knot as she remembered a baby, so tiny, so precious.

Where is he now, Lord?

"Giselle and I aren't visitors this time." The tightness in Jack's voice made her curious. "We're moving to Churchill permanently. I bought a hotel."

"You're the new owner of the Northern Lights Lodge," she said in sudden understanding.

"Yes." He didn't exactly look thrilled.

"You aren't excited about your venture? Do you have lots of experience?" She wished she could make herself small enough so his broad shoulder didn't keep brushing hers, but that was not easy when she was five foot eight.

"No. I was a cop in Vancouver." His voice hummed

with a low rumble. "It's all I ever wanted to be and I was good at it."

A cop who loved shoes? She'd think about that later.

"I lived in Vancouver once." Alicia couldn't quite suppress a shudder. "Why'd you quit being a cop to run a hotel?" she asked, then realized how nosy she sounded. To change the subject she said, "You'll probably regret leaving mild Vancouver when winter returns to Churchill."

"I doubt it." Jack said it with a bald fierceness, his gaze on his daughter. "I'm moving for Giselle, to keep her safe." His jaw clenched and a tiny tic appeared.

"Oh. Is she in danger?" Alicia couldn't contain her curiosity about this obviously hurting man and his very cute daughter.

"Maybe." He gave Alicia the kind of look that sized her up in about three seconds. "Her mom was an internal-affairs cop. We thought she'd be safer there than on the street. Turns out we were wrong. Simone was killed by a dirty cop two years ago."

"I'm so sorry." Alicia's heart winced at the grief that colored his voice. "So you're left to take care of Giselle on your own. But you can't do that if you're working as a cop, so you bought the hotel," she guessed. "Good for you."

"And because Laurel's here in Churchill. She's the only family we have left." Jack's gaze drifted to the other passengers, who were settling into a drowsy state as spring's twilight faded and darkness fluttered over the land.

Then he faced her, a line of strain deepening around his mouth. His blue eyes turned navy. Alicia felt the tension emanating from him.

"I'll do anything to protect Giselle," he said in a fierce voice. "Including figuring out a new occupation. It helps that Laurel has a friend who is a megahotelier. His name is Teddy Stonechild and he comes to Churchill a lot. He promised to help me get the place up and running."

"Giselle will be safe in Churchill. We're so isolated that most of the world barely knows we exist," Alicia said, trying to lighten the mood.

"I hope that's not true." A smile tried to play with the corner of Jack's mouth. "Otherwise, my hotel will go broke."

"Highly unlikely. Teddy knows everything about running a hotel. He should, given how many he has." Alicia shrugged. "Anyway, the polar bear seekers book every available room from mid-September to November, the northern lights hunters come in January and February, and we get a lot of folks stopping by to see the belugas from now till fall. Lodging in Churchill is very limited and very relaxed, so I'm sure you'll do well."

"I hope so." The words emerged in a quiet mur-

mur as Jack stared at his daughter. "Because failure is not an option."

"I'll say a prayer for you and Giselle," she offered.

"I doubt that will make a difference." His voice hardened. "God abandoned us when He let Simone die."

"God doesn't abandon His children." Alicia bristled under the look Jack gave her, a look that said he thought she was being childish. "Believe me, I know."

"Why? Do you have kids?" Jack asked.

"I'm single," she said firmly. Then, lest he think she was angling for a date, she added, "And I intend to stay that way."

"Not exactly what I asked." His gaze narrowed. "But I agree with you. I intend to stay single, too."

"Oh?" A hunk like him staying single? In Churchill? Alicia almost laughed.

"I will never allow myself to go through losing someone I care for again." The absolute loss in Jack's voice killed her amusement. When he spoke again, his voice was more even. "If you had kids, you'd understand how they become the focus of your life. You'll do anything for them. Giselle is my world. Besides her, nothing else matters."

I do understand what you mean, Jack. I know exactly how you feel. I'd do anything to keep my son safe. But I don't know where he is, or how to find him.

"Sorry, guess I'm not very good company to-night," Jack muttered turning away. The keep-away signs were clearly posted. Only natural, given he'd lost his wife.

Not that Alicia was interested in Jack. The idea of a relationship with any man scared her. That was her legacy from Vancouver. After the attack she'd never felt safe there, so she'd come to isolated Churchill, got a job and eventually, with the help of her dear friends, she'd bought her store.

Churchill was Alicia's escape from the ugliness of her past.

Minutes passed. She felt Jack's occasional scrutiny but kept staring out the window. She didn't want to talk anymore. Not now that the dark curtain of memories had fallen around her. Her heart ached with the same old longing—to know her child was safe, loved, cared for. If only God would answer that prayer.

Not that Alicia had any right to ask a thing of God. Giving her son away when he was most vulnerable made her unworthy of motherhood.

But I was vulnerable, too, her heart cried. *I didn't know I'd never see him again. Don't let him grow up alone and scared like I was, Lord. Please keep him safe.*

Her cell phone vibrated. She snapped it open. "Hello."

"It's me. Listen, Alicia, there's something you

must know. Jeremy Parcet has been asking questions about you." Nancy Runningbear's voice was as clear as if she was seated beside Alicia in the train instead of miles away in Vancouver. "He's been looking up kids who were in your class, asking them where you are, what you're doing, stuff like that."

"M-Mr. Parcet is?" Terror stole Alicia's breath. "Why?"

"His father died. Apparently there's a stipulation in his will that Jeremy must show proof of an heir within three years or he can't inherit." Her old friend paused. "I was told Jeremy's wife can't have children," she murmured.

Alicia's throat choked with fear.

"My guess is he's done some research, knows you got pregnant after he attacked you and is now after the child." Nancy harrumphed her disgust. "I thought you should know."

"Thank you." The words came out in a whisper.

"Don't thank me. That man was someone you trusted, your teacher for goodness' sake. He should be in jail for what he did to you." Nancy paused. Alicia could hear Nancy's husband's voice in the background. "Harold's telling me to get to the point which is, if Jeremy can prove he's a father, he'll be able to inherit. It's around four million, Alicia, very big motivation to find you. Once he does, he'll turn up and press for details about your child. You have to be careful."

"Yes." Fear clamped a band around the back of Alicia's neck. "I appreciate your warning, Nancy," she murmured, checking over one shoulder to be certain no one was listening. "I'll always be grateful for the way you and Harold took me in back then. I don't know what I'd have done without you."

"God would have provided someone else," Nancy assured her, her voice cracking. "He always does. We're just happy He used us. I have to go now. You be careful."

"I will. Thanks for the heads up. Bye."

Alicia stared into the darkness outside while she absorbed what she'd heard. The wheels clicked over the tracks in a rhythmic motion that had apparently lulled Jack to sleep. She peeked over at him again. The man was certainly handsome. But she couldn't think about his looks or the way his raspy voice made her skin tingle.

The same ten-year-old prayer sighed from Alicia's heart. Surely God would answer soon. Surely this time He'd protect her from Mr. Parcet. If not her, because she'd failed to be the mother she should have, then surely for her innocent child.

She'd let herself imagine expanding her business, but she ought to know that God didn't give people like her their dreams. That was for better people, people who didn't make terrible mistakes like giving away their child.

But the past didn't matter now. She had to concentrate on finding her son, on making certain he was safe and loved. And far away from Jeremy Parcet, her rapist.

Again Alicia's gaze rested on Jack. He'd been a detective. Maybe— No! Asking him for help would mean revealing her past. She could imagine the disgust she'd see in those blue eyes.

No. She'd have to handle this herself.

Chapter Two

Painful prickles woke Jack around three-thirty. He tried to shift his sleeping arm but a weight held him down. Waking more fully, he peered through the darkness at the woman whose head rested against his shoulder.

She reminded him of the Indian maiden in that show Giselle used to love when she was little. Pocahontas. Only Alicia Featherstone was prettier. Those high, defined cheekbones and straight, proud nose proclaimed her Native Canadian ancestry. Her hair, almost black as a raven's wing, was bound in thick braids and tied at the ends by strings of leather woven with turquoise beads. Thick bangs fringed her broad forehead ending just above arched black eyebrows.

Though her eyes were closed, he knew they were a rich espresso that turned black when she was upset. Lush lashes rested on dusky cheekbones. Her full lips pursed as she gave a tiny shiver and shifted her head to a more comfortable position against his shoulder.

Alicia wore no rings. She'd said she was single, which Laurel had told him in passing. His sister had also mentioned that Alicia had planned a big summer project for the Lives Under Construction boys—building a sod house like the Cree Indians would have used when the first settlers came to Churchill. As soon as Laurel had been certain he was moving to Churchill, she'd asked Jack to help.

Alicia doesn't know the meaning of overdoing, his sister had told him. *Nothing stops her from giving her all. She's what Mom used to call a giver. She thinks she can accomplish anything she sets her mind to.*

Not a bad thing to believe. He'd hidden his chagrin at Laurel's request. *You think she's in over her head?*

No, but a whole house? It's too much for her. I know you and Simone volunteered with the restoration work on that sod building at the museum in Vancouver. You must have picked up some knowledge. Laurel had pinned him with her gaze. *The boys are really looking forward to this, Jack. They're planning a community celebration when it's finished, to show off their handiwork. You'll help Alicia, won't you?*

If I have time, Jack had finally agreed. *Running*

*the hotel is going to be a steep learning curve, sis.
It's not something I've ever done.*

It won't be like running a big-city hotel. Laurel
had chuckled. *Anyway Teddy will be here for the
whole summer to help. He's grooming his son to take
over his hotel empire. Teddy wants to give him time
to manage on his own. With an expert like him to
teach you, you'll have lots of time for Alicia.*

That's when Jack had noticed something in his
sister's voice, something that he had to nip in the
bud.

Don't matchmake, Laurel, he'd warned. *Don't
even consider it. I'm not interested in anyone. At
all. Ever.*

Ever? Laurel had smiled sympathetically. *I know
Simone's death hit both you and Giselle hard. Give
it a little more time.*

More time? For what? It felt as if he'd barely
survived the past two years. Jack was pretty sure
more time wouldn't heal the gaping hole in his heart.
Simone had been his high school sweetheart. They'd
done everything together. They'd been soul mates.
That only happened once in a lifetime and God had
ended it.

Now Giselle would be the focus of his world.

"I'm sorry. I didn't mean to crush you." The soft
apology broke through his thoughts as Alicia jerked
away. Cool air chilled his arm where her warm

cheek had rested. Her face bore a flush of embarrassment. "Please excuse me."

"No problem." He rotated his shoulder, trying to ignore her scrutiny through the shadows. It didn't work. He subconsciously noticed every detail about her. Not because he was interested, he told himself. Just a habit left over from his law-enforcement days.

"Are you all right?" she whispered.

"I'm not used to sitting so long." His nose twitched at the scent she wore. He'd noticed it earlier. Something dried and earthy, like an herb. Sage? "Are you full-blooded Cree?"

"Yes." She looked a bit surprised at his sudden question but didn't volunteer any more. Instead, she averted her eyes as if hiding something.

"Where do your parents live?" Why did he feel compelled to learn more about her?

"They died when I was thirteen." Alicia faced him, her eyes darkening to black diamonds. "My dad was a pilot. They were returning from visiting a friend up north when their plane crashed. I was sent to live in Vancouver with a distant relative." Her gaze challenged him. *Any other questions?*

"I didn't mean to pry," he apologized.

"It's not a secret. Anyone in Churchill could have told you the same thing," she said.

But Jack was pretty sure they couldn't tell him any other details about Alicia Featherstone. According to

Laurel, she kept to herself. He guessed most people respected the resolute barriers she wore like shields.

"Can I ask *you* a question?" Alicia murmured.

"I guess." He waited warily, hoping she didn't have the wrong impression. Alicia was very pretty but he wasn't interested.

Liar.

"What's with the boots?" Her gaze fell to his feet.

"You don't like them?" Jack held out one foot, admiring the feel of the supple leather snuggled against his toes without pinching.

"They're great. Very, uh, pretty." She wrinkled her nose. "It's just that you don't strike me as the pretty type."

"Thanks." Jack smothered his chuckle when she dipped her head. "It's not about fashion. I do—did," he corrected gloomily, "a lot of work on my feet. I decided early on that I wasn't going to be a literal flatfoot so I bought good shoes."

"You do realize they'll be ruined in Churchill?" she warned. "You must have noticed on previous visits that we only have pavement in some places. Other streets are gravel. The worst roads around town are dirt. If you wear those on the beach, the stones will poke through the soles and you'll suffer a lot worse than flat feet." She thrust out her own foot. "Trust me. You will end up in ordinary hiking boots, just like the rest of us."

"Never." He liked her dare-you attitude. "Tell me about your store."

"Tansi?" She frowned, leaned her head to one side. "I told you. I gather First Nations work from all across Canada, some of it very unusual. I try to sell it with bits of history attached, to give tourists perspective on how the piece came to be, what it means to our culture."

Jack noted how a sparkle lit up her eyes as she spoke. It was clear Alicia loved her work. He paid close attention as she continued.

"There's a lot of prejudice toward Native Canadians." Her chin thrust out as if to defend her people. "I'm trying to create a bridge by showing and teaching the values in our culture. I want to help people appreciate the meaning of their purchase."

"What kinds of things do you sell?" He wanted to keep her talking. She intrigued him. Surprising when nothing had really interested him for ages.

"My stock changes constantly. There are no two things alike. At the moment I have an Inuit carving of a walrus, very tiny but perfectly detailed. A woman makes beaded slippers with real rabbit fur trim for my shop. She lives entirely off the land. This trip I restocked silver and beaded earrings made by a village elder who is wheelchair-bound but the most creative lady you'll ever meet." Alicia shrugged. "I also have some paintings of the northern lights, knitting that's been dyed from local plants, photos of the area. All kinds of things."

"And I'm sure the polar bears are represented, too," he teased.

"Of course. Bears are an important part of Cree culture," she said.

"Do *you* make any of these crafts?"

"I'm not really talented in that way." The light in her eyes faded to a dull mud tone. "I never had much time to learn the old ways because I was taken from my community when my parents died."

"Were you adopted?" he asked, curiosity growing.

"No. I was thirteen. Adoptive parents want babies or very young kids." She frowned at him. "Why did you ask that?"

"Just wondering." But Jack knew he couldn't shut down like that. He'd poked into her life; turnabout was fair play. Besides, he needed help to figure out his next move. "Giselle is adopted. My wife wanted to keep it a secret as long as she could. I didn't agree but Simone was adamant. Then she died. I thought I'd tell Giselle when she turned sixteen."

"But she found out first?" Alicia guessed.

"Yes." His lips tightened into a line. "Two months ago she found her mother's old diary and figured out we weren't her birth parents."

"It happens." Alicia didn't say any more but somehow Jack felt her empathy.

"She's really angry that we didn't tell her." He

sighed. "That's natural, I guess. But she keeps demanding more information about her birth family."

"And you don't want to tell her?" Disapproval laced her voice.

"I can't tell her more because I don't know any more." Jack's jaw clenched. Why had he started this?

Alicia leaned against the window of the train, her gaze on him.

"I have so little information." He raked a hand through his hair as helplessness gripped him. "There's nothing to go on. Simone insisted on a closed adoption. That means that Giselle can't find out anything more than what we already know until she's eighteen. Then she can request the adoption agency in British Columbia to open her file."

"Normal procedure."

Jack nodded. Did Alicia know about adoptions? If she did, maybe she could talk to Giselle, help her understand it wasn't his fault he couldn't get the answers she wanted.

"I'm assuming her birth father's name wasn't listed or is a dead end?" Alicia asked.

He nodded. "Dead end."

"But surely you have the name of the biological mother on Giselle's birth certificate?" Her head tilted to one side as she studied him. "You were a police officer. You must have a lot of contacts. Couldn't someone track the name?"

He didn't want to answer but Alicia kept waiting.

"I did track her." Jack sighed. "Two years after the adoption, Giselle's birth mother disappeared. There's no trace of her." Oddly, it felt good to discuss this with her.

"What about Laurel? Surely as a former social worker, your sister could—"

"Social workers are provincial employees," he explained. "Laurel never worked in that province."

"I see." Alicia fell silent, apparently lost in thought.

"Can I ask you something?" Jack waited until she nodded. "How do you know about adoptions? You said you were never adopted so—" He let it hang, his curiosity about her growing.

"I wasn't." Her gaze moved to one side, avoiding his. "I, um, for a long time I've been looking for someone who was adopted. But the clues I had led to dead ends. I don't have connections like you do so I don't know where to look next."

"My connections weren't much help," Jack told her. He dug in his pocket and pulled out the slip of paper he'd been carrying around since his last day of work. "But this might be. Someone gave me this website address. They said it's been helpful to others. It wasn't for me, but you're welcome to copy the address and check it out."

"I, um, don't have a pen or paper," she said after a moment's hesitation.

"I do." Jack pulled out the small pad and pen he

always kept in his breast pocket and held them out. "Old habit from my detective days." Surprisingly she didn't take, either. "You already know about this site?"

"No." Her cheeks darkened. "This is embarrassing. You see, I have really bad eyesight and my glasses are in the bag you put up top. Would you mind copying it out for me?"

"I can get the bag," he offered, shifting to rise.

"No, no. Don't stir yourself." She laid her hand on his arm. "You'll wake up someone." She jerked her hand away. "If you could write it down for me, I'd be grateful."

"Sure. Okay." He scribbled down the web address, tore out the sheet and handed it to her.

"Thank you." Alicia studied it for a moment then folded it and tucked it into her jeans pocket. "I'll take a look when I get home."

"I hope it helps."

When Alicia merely smiled at him before turning her face to the window, Jack understood that was all the conversation she wanted for now. Suited him. He didn't want her to think he was trying to get too friendly. He checked on Giselle then pulled his e-reader from the seat pocket in front and flicked it on.

But the novel couldn't hold Jack's interest. Instead he got hung up thinking about the woman next to him. There was something about Alicia Featherstone that intrigued him and it wasn't only her quick rush to defend God.

Though she'd been friendly enough, she had a quality about her that said *no trespassing.* She seemed to not need anyone else. Self-contained, that was it.

Jack couldn't help wondering why. Alicia was lovely to look at, had a nice figure and ran her own independent business. She appeared to have her life together. And yet when she'd crashed into him earlier, she'd jerked back, ready to protect herself. He remembered how she'd ordered him to let go of her arm. She'd tensed—an automatic response to a perceived threat.

Because she'd had to defend herself before?

As he'd told Laurel, Jack wasn't interested in a romantic relationship with anyone. But his detective background made Alicia's almost bristling reaction interesting, as had her response when he'd asked if she had kids. Suddenly Jack could think of a hundred questions to ask the lovely Indian woman.

She's nothing to do with you. You and Giselle are on your own. Even if you could forget what you and Simone shared, are you really willing to risk loving again and losing again?

No.

In a rush, the lost, empty feeling he'd battled for two long years returned. He'd barely survived the pain of Simone's death and that was only because of Giselle, because he was determined not to lose her, too.

Alicia Featherstone might become his coworker on the kids' project, but that's all she could ever be. He would not contemplate loving and losing again.

Jack twisted in his seat so his back was to Alicia. He forced himself to read the words on his screen. But despite his best intentions, every so often his glance slipped to the silent woman in the seat next to his.

Though he was tired, sleep evaded him.

Given his curiosity about Alicia Featherstone, he should probably refuse to work with her. But he wasn't going to. He had too many questions that demanded answers.

Chapter Three

Alicia awoke feeling watched.

Sure enough, when she peeked through her lashes she found a dark brown gaze fixed on her. Self-conscious and disheveled, she swallowed and tried to think of what to say to Jack's daughter.

"You snore." Giselle flopped into the seat her father had obviously vacated while Alicia was asleep. "Delicately, but still. It's snoring."

"Good morning." Alicia gave her a pointed look. "My name is Alicia Featherstone. And you're Giselle, I understand. It's nice to meet you."

"Yeah." The girl flicked her long hair over one shoulder. "I guess that was rude."

Ignoring her unrepentant stare, Alicia said nothing. She pulled a brush from her purse, undid her braids and combed out her hair before swirling it into a topknot on her head.

"Sorry." Giselle didn't sound the least bit sorry.

"I hear you're moving to Churchill," Alicia said, cutting her some slack.

"So Jack says." The chip on Giselle's shoulder was huge.

"Jack?" Alicia tamped down her irritation at this cheeky child.

"Well, I can't really call him Dad, now can I?" Giselle snapped in a sour tone.

"Why not?" *Spoiled,* Alicia thought to herself.

Yet her heart ached for the confused girl. Giselle's world had been rocked, first by her mom's death and then by learning nothing she'd believed about her family was true. Moving away from all that was familiar couldn't be easy, either.

"Jack hasn't been your dad for all these years?" she asked gently.

"Yes." Giselle whooshed out a breath that blew her bangs all over. "He has. He's been a really good father and I love him a lot. That's why this is so hard. He lied to me."

"I didn't lie, Giselle." Jack stood in the aisle. His face conveyed his hurt.

"Lied by omission then." She jumped up and held out a hand. "Can I have some money to buy breakfast?"

"I guess I'm your father enough for that, huh?" Jack muttered with a sideways glance at his daughter. She simply shrugged. He transferred the two cups he carried into one hand then fished several bills out of his shirt pocket and handed them over. Giselle flounced away. "Nothing for me, thanks," he muttered, staring longingly at her departing figure.

"Preteen. It's a horrible age," Alicia consoled. "She'll get over it."

"Soon, I hope." He held out a lidded cup. "Coffee. I figured you could use some. You look great, but it wasn't the most restful night I've ever had."

"Thank you." She accepted the cup, freezing for a moment when his warm fingers brushed hers. "Maybe I'm used to these chairs because I've ridden the train so often."

"To get your store stock?"

"Uh-huh. The sleeper cars are always booked far in advance. Since I'm never sure when I'll be on the train, I always sleep in the chairs," she explained. "I don't mind traveling at this time of year. The landscape is amazing. Seeing spring arrive from the train is far more interesting than watching snow drift in winter." She sipped her coffee, enjoying the rich dark flavor. "Thank you for this."

"Sure. My sister told me about a project you're planning for her Lives boys. That's what locals call her rehabilitation center, right?"

"Yes." Alicia nodded. "It's a shortened version of Lives Under Construction, which we use to refer to the army barracks she's renovated, the outbuildings and all the land around."

"I thought so." Jack sat down, stretching his legs

in front. "So—a sod house, right? Laurel asked me to help."

"She did?" Alicia stared at him. "I didn't know that." She shook her head, uneasy at the prospect of having Jack nearby, watching her. "You don't have to bother. We'll manage. The boys are very responsible."

"I'm sure they are. But I promised and I don't break my promises to Laurel, ever. She's the older sister and she makes me pay," he teased. Then a frown flickered across his face. "It sounds like you don't want my help."

"It's not that." She bit her bottom lip, struggling to rephrase the truth.

"Don't worry, Alicia. I know how to take directions." He chuckled when she couldn't mask her dubious expression. "I'll help, but the hotel will have to come first." He tipped his head to one side, studying her. "How did you come up with the sod house idea anyway?"

"From a display I saw." She leaned her back against the window to put as much distance between them as possible. She would have moved across the aisle if Giselle hadn't left her things scattered over both seats.

Oddly enough, Jack's nearness didn't make Alicia feel unsafe and it wasn't just that he was a cop and also Laurel's brother. Jack was still grieving for his wife. She couldn't imagine he was the type to try to take advantage of her here on a public train. But mostly she wasn't worried because he'd emphasized that he intended to remain single.

Still, his nearness caused a nervousness deep inside her that Alicia didn't understand.

"What kind of a display?" Jack asked.

"It was held inside a caribou tent and it was amazing." She tried to explain but cut it short when his eyes began to glaze. "Anyway, the presenters were descendants of an original settlement family. Their elder told stories about how their ancestors built sod houses to live in. I thought it would be fun to build one as a summer project for the boys. Kyle Loness—he's the activities director at Lives—and Rick Salinger, our minister, have both promised to help."

"Sounds interesting. Do you have a book about it, or plans?" Jack asked.

"No," Alicia answered, slewing her eyes to the window, though there was nothing unusual in the muskeg pushing up to reveal the permafrost beneath. "All I have is a rough sketch an elder drew for me."

"Well, I guess you could get the library to order some books." Jack savored his coffee, his face thoughtful. "You can't just go out and start digging. You'll need some kind of plan."

Alicia gulped, because that was exactly what she'd intended to do—start digging as soon as the town allocated the land. Now she realized how silly that was. Of course they would need a plan. Houses were built in stages.

Rattled by the thought of being asked to consult a book, she knew she'd have to be careful or else Jack and the rest of Churchill would discover she couldn't read very well. Her mother had tried to teach her when their remote village lost its teacher, but her English hadn't been great. When she'd been moved to Vancouver, Alicia had struggled and failed to catch up.

"Since you'll be helping us, perhaps you wouldn't mind contacting the library," she said, crossing her fingers that he'd accept.

"I guess I could." His forehead furrowed, he plied her with questions.

Alicia answered as best she could but his proximity unnerved her. She was grateful when Giselle finally returned.

"I hope you don't mind if I ask this." The girl stood in the aisle, leaning against the seat in front. "You're an Indian, aren't you?"

Jack choked on his coffee then glared at Giselle, clearly aggravated by her impudence.

"Native Canadian Indian, yes." Alicia held her gaze as she said the words proudly, refusing to back down. "Why?"

"One of my teachers said you often have names that have special meanings."

"You're asking if Alicia is a traditional Native name?" she said.

"Yes, like *Piapot*." Giselle frowned. "Do you know what that name means?"

"One who knows the secrets of the Sioux." She hid her smile as Giselle's eyes brightened. "I'm sorry to disappoint you. I'm afraid I'm just plain Alicia Featherstone."

"Well, at least you have Featherstone, though I don't know what meaning that could have. Feathers and stones are complete opposites," Giselle complained.

"Sorry." Alicia hid her smile. "If you're interested in learning about Chief Piapot, every Thursday night I lead a campfire at Lives. I tell the boys stories of Native history. You're welcome to join us."

"Thanks." Giselle's smile lit up her face. She returned to her seat across the aisle. Moments later she was busy on her pink cell phone.

"I'm sorry," Jack apologized. "Sometimes I have no clue what will come out of her mouth. I'm not sure she does, either."

Alicia burst out laughing. "Forget it. That in-your-face attitude is what makes kids so refreshing."

"I'll try to remember that," he said drily. "Hey, we're slowing down."

"Yes. We'll arrive in Churchill soon." She smiled. "Did I ever thank you for rescuing my packages?"

"I wouldn't want Tansi's stock to go missing." He

studied her for a moment. "I don't know much about your kind of business, but Laurel says you're doing very well. Have you ever considered expanding? There's a much bigger market outside of Churchill that could use some education about your culture."

Warmth exploded inside her. At last, someone who thought like her. She gazed at Jack with admiration.

"I dream about having a second store, maybe in Winnipeg, but I haven't worked out how to do it." Alicia hesitated, realizing she'd just shared her dream with a total stranger, a dream no one else knew about. Why was it so easy to talk to Jack?

Just as quickly her excitement drained away. There was no point in thinking about future expansion with him or anyone else. People like her with no sources of funding didn't have second or third stores. And now that Mr. Parcet was asking questions about her, it was only a matter of time before he'd show up to get information. He wasn't going to get it from her, of course, but she had to put her dreams on hold and concentrate on making sure her son was safe before Mr. Parcet found her.

How do I do that, God, when I don't know where he is?

Alicia stared out the window, lost in ways and means she might employ. The first thing would be to talk to the social worker she'd been assigned when she was fifteen and had given up her son. What was her name? Mrs. End-something. Endecott? Enderby? Endersley, that was it. She silently repeated the name to fix it in her mind.

"I want to talk to Alicia, Dad. Can we change seats for a while?"

Alicia blinked out of her thoughts and found Jack studying her. He raised one eyebrow.

"Do you mind speaking with Giselle?" he said. "It's okay if you'd rather rest."

"She's not old, Dad. She doesn't have to rest." Scorn laced Giselle's shrill tone.

"Actually I've been up for about thirty-six hours and I am a bit tired, *Jack*." Alicia smiled at him, deliberately cutting Giselle out of the conversation. She felt sorry for the child, but she wanted to make a point to Giselle to curb her attitude.

"I'm sorry." Giselle was a quick study. She looked remorseful as she shook her head. "You must be exhausted. It's just that I'm curious about those stories you mentioned. Will you tell me more?"

Wasn't her life goal to bring awareness and knowledge to the world about her culture? Alicia nodded. "I guess we could talk for a while, if your father is agreeable."

"As long as you are." Jack waited for Alicia's nod. He gave her a quizzical smile before he rose and moved across the aisle.

Giselle sat down in the seat he vacated. She fiddled with her hands for a few moments before she looked at Alicia. "My mother would have been furious if she'd heard me be rude," she admitted.

"And you want to get back at her for dying, or something?" Alicia frowned.

"No." Giselle shook her head.

"Your father then?" And here she'd thought preteens would be easy to understand. Alicia took a shot anyway. "You blame your dad."

"For Mom's death?" Giselle frowned and shook her head again. "I don't blame him but—"

"You want him to pay," Alicia said in sudden understanding.

"I want my life back the way it was," the girl said fiercely with a sideways glance at her dad, who had his nose buried between two black covers. "I want my mom."

"I know you do. But that isn't going to happen, Giselle, and I think you know it." Alicia kept her tone gentle. "I doubt your dad likes the way things are any better than you, but don't forget he lost someone, too. I'm sure he's doing the very best he can."

"It's not enough." Tears filled Giselle's dark eyes. "Aunt Laurel says I need to talk to God about it, but I'm mad at God, too." She wrapped her arms around her middle and thrust out her chin. "I feel mad at just about everyone."

"I understand." Alicia laid her hand on the girl's shoulder. "Maybe this won't help much right now, but things *will* get better. Eventually. God has wonderful things planned for you."

"You think?" Giselle stared at her, her big brown eyes begging for confirmation.

"I *know*. There's a verse in Psalms that I sometimes repeat to myself. It says, 'Weeping may endure for the night but joy comes in the morning.'"

"My mom had something like that written in one of her diaries," Giselle murmured. She was silent for a long time before she brushed away a tear and rose. "I really do want to hear your stories, Alicia, but maybe you and I could talk another time. Excuse me." Then she scooted across the aisle.

"I don't know what you said," Jack said when he eventually returned to the seat beside Alicia. "But thank you. Giselle apologized to me."

"Don't thank me. You have a lovely daughter." Alicia shared a smile with him, but it lasted a second too long and that made her stomach clench. This man had an odd effect on her and she didn't know why. She ducked away from his gaze. "We're coming into the station," she said. "Would you mind giving me my things you put up top? I'll pull out my sweater and try to stuff the packages into the backpack so you can have your bag back."

"Keep it. You can return it next time we see each other," he said. Once the train stopped, Jack rose, lifted down her bags and handed them to her. "I'm looking forward to working with you on that sod house, Alicia." His blue gaze sent a tiny spark wiggling up her spine.

"Me, too." Funny thing was she meant it.

Alicia stepped off the train and quickly made her way through the station and outside, anxious to get away from Jack's disturbing presence so she could figure out her odd reaction. A soft spring wind blew across her skin, chasing away the odd tremors she'd felt when she stood so close to him. The fresh air revitalized her. How wonderful to come home.

Then she remembered. Mr. Parcet.

After a furtive glance over one shoulder Alicia hurried toward her shop, checking every so often to be sure he wasn't nearby. Of course he wasn't, she chastised herself. He hadn't been on the train. But the worry clung nonetheless.

It was silly, but Alicia gave a sigh of relief as she unlocked the store door and stepped safely inside. She turned the sign to Open, switched on the lights and then strode to the back, where she set down the bag Jack had lent her.

She climbed the stairs to her apartment above the shop, pausing to toss her backpack into her bedroom and wash the tiredness from her face. After snatching a carton of juice and a muffin from the fridge, she hurried downstairs, eager to unpack her wares. She forced herself to eat slowly as anticipation built about the treasures she'd picked up on her trip.

Alicia had barely removed the first box when the door opened.

"Giselle and I are going out to Lives tonight for supper," Jack said, holding up his phone. "Laurel says you're welcome, too."

"That's kind of you but perhaps another time," Alicia declined.

"Okay. See you." Jack raised his hand in a wave then left as quickly as he'd come. Alicia ignored her accelerated heartbeat as she dragged her gaze off his retreating figure.

What was wrong with her?

After one last sip of juice she washed her hands, then tenderly pushed away the protective tissue paper so she could lift out the first treasure. In her palms she cradled the chiseled figure of a woman with a baby papoose strapped to her back. Mother and child. Alicia let her mind drift back almost ten years.

Her son. Even now the scent of him returned, soft, sweet, a miracle. Tiny, delicate limbs, so small yet so perfectly formed. Her heart hiccupped as she remembered one pink finger reaching up to brush her cheek, as if he knew who she was, as if he was asking her to rethink her decision to give him away.

Tears rolled over her cheeks as the sadness Alicia had kept tamped down would no longer stay buried. She hated everything that brought him into being, but she'd never hated him. She couldn't. He was beautiful, innocent and so full of promise. He didn't deserve hate. He deserved love, a chance to push his way into the world, to prove that everything was not dirty and evil and messed up. He deserved happiness. Alicia had known she couldn't give him that.

"Alicia?" Jack stood in the doorway again, staring at her. How was it she hadn't heard the tinkle of the bell signaling the opening door?

She turned away, scrubbed a hand across her cheek then set the figure carefully in the box before she looked at him. "Yes?"

"Are you okay?" he asked in that already familiar low, rumbling voice.

"Fine. Just touched by the beauty of this piece." She glanced at the sculpture, then folded her hands together lest he see their trembling. "Is there something you need?"

He cleared his voice but said nothing. His scrutiny continued. Finally she forced herself to look directly at him.

"I just wanted to tell you that I think it'll take me at least a week of steady focus on the hotel before I can even think about working on the sod house." He sounded hesitant. Was he regretting his offer of help?

"That's fine," she said to give him an out. "It's only May. The kids won't be finished school until the end of June anyway. There's plenty of time."

"Oh." His blue eyes searched hers with an intensity she couldn't stand.

Alicia rushed to remove the other boxes from the mesh bag. Then she walked toward him, holding it out. "Thanks for lending me this."

"You're welcome." He took the bag from her. "I know it's none of my business and this probably isn't the time, but I've been wondering how you first came to Churchill."

"I came here looking for someone," she said after a moment of quick thought. She could hardly tell him she'd been following a lead Nancy's private investigator had found regarding her child. It didn't matter anyway. "I didn't find them."

"But you stayed anyway?" he said, one eyebrow raised.

"After some persuasion." She needed to frame her words carefully so she didn't give too much away. "Do you know Lucy Clow?"

"Small woman, white-haired? She and her husband were missionaries to the Inuit?" he muttered, his forehead pleated. "I think she helps Laurel's cook at Lives sometimes."

"Lucy helps everyone, whether they want it or not," Alicia said with a grin. "Anyway, an older couple owned this store, but they wanted to take a trip to see their son in Australia. Lucy was their bookkeeper. She suggested I help here until they returned. She showed me how things worked and got them to fix up the rooms above for me to live in."

Her home. Alicia still savored the small sanctuary she'd found. But she could hardly tell him that.

"So they didn't come back?" Jack drawled.

"Oh, yes. But just long enough to pack. They moved to be near their son. The community didn't want the store to close because it was such a good tourist stop. Since the owners wanted to leave, they and the community worked out a no-interest loan for me to buy the store." She fiddled with an arrangement on a side table. "A couple of friends staked me and Lucy helped me fill out government grant forms. And here I am." She held out her arms. "This is my third year running Tansi."

"Good for you." Jack kept staring at her for a long time. Alicia shifted under that intense stare, relieved when he checked his watch. "Giselle will kill me. I told her I'd be back with the truck to pick up our stuff. That was ages ago. See you."

Alicia nodded and held a smile in place until the door closed behind him. Then she let out a sigh and pushed away all tantalizing thoughts of the handsome policeman as she continued unpacking her treasures in between clients.

When her last customer had left, she went into the back room and started the coffeemaker. She glanced at the wall clock and sent a quiet prayer heavenward for Nancy and Harold Runningbear. They'd taught her to tell time and do basic addition and subtraction. Without them…she wouldn't think about that.

But even Nancy hadn't been able to teach her to read or write beyond the most basic level. Alicia was sure it was because there was something wrong with her.

If only…

Alicia shook off the nagging thoughts. More than anyone, she knew how pointless it was to wish the past had never happened.

Focusing her mind on her work, she noticed it was almost three o'clock. Eli, a boy from Lives Under Construction who helped out at Tansi after school, would arrive in about twenty minutes. Alicia needed to decide what she wanted on the tags for her new items so he could write them up, which meant she'd have to think of another excuse for not doing it herself. Being illiterate was bad enough, but keeping it a secret was even harder. And she had to keep it under wraps, or else she'd risk becoming the town's laughingstock or activate worry that she might not be able to repay the community loan.

She regretted now that she'd let someone else do her homework in school, that she'd allowed herself to believe that quitting school to live on the streets was an option. When Nancy and Harold had taken her in, they'd helped her see she could start over, make something of her life. But Mr. Parcet's attack had made returning to the special literacy classes impossible. She hadn't been able to go back there, couldn't be anywhere near him or any other man without panicking. Then she'd learned she was pregnant.

How ironic that she still thought of him as *Mr.,* a respect unworthy of him. But to think of him otherwise was to admit he had a personal part in her life. Alicia couldn't allow that. Nor could she again relive those terror-filled moments.

She wasn't that dumb fifteen-year-old girl anymore. Look how far she'd come in ten years. She had her own business to run. She had a life. She was stronger and more determined than ever. She could figure out a way to protect her child, too. Somehow.

Alicia picked up the picture Lucy Clow had left on her desk. Sweet Lucy did the books for Alicia's business but she also ran the store whenever Alicia was away. Though Lucy and her husband, Hector, were retired missionaries to the Inuit, they were by no means retired. Lucy acted as part-time church secretary, frequently helped out at Lives Under Construction and stepped in anywhere else in Churchill where she saw a need.

In Alicia, Lucy obviously saw a need. Though Alicia had never confessed, Lucy seemed to know that Alicia couldn't read much and she made allowances. One of those allowances was the pictures she left for Alicia, to apprise her of something. This one seemed to be saying that Jim Deerfoot had more antler carvings to sell. That was good because Alicia's stock was low.

Lucy's presence at Tansi yesterday meant that everything in the store had been thoroughly dusted, the sales records updated and the storeroom organized in extreme detail. Tomorrow Lucy would stop by and explain the accounts, what had sold, what was in the bank. It was her assistance that kept Tansi in the black. Lucy was like a revered grandmother in Alicia's heart. Alicia adored the sprightly woman whose faith in God held strong and firm in the face of hardship.

Lucy had even made the upstairs apartment glow. The woman loved to clean and organize. She'd done such a good job while Alicia was away that all she needed was a few groceries. She'd just finished making a mental list when Eli sauntered in.

"Hey," she greeted. "How are you?"

"Awesome." Eli's attention immediately honed in on the items she'd brought with her. "These rock," he said, bending to inspect each one. "Like totally sick."

"Sick?" Alarmed, Alicia stared at him. "What do you mean?"

"Sick, as in great, Alicia," he said in a droll tone.

"Oh. Well, I'm glad you like them." Once he'd stored his backpack, she explained what she wanted him to create for the tags on each item. "Make them special, okay? You're a genius when it comes to writing these tags," she praised, "so I know you'll do a totally sick job." She giggled when he rolled his eyes. "I have to get groceries. My fridge is empty."

"Go ahead. Let this genius get to work." Eli

flexed his fingers, pulled out his label supplies, then stopped. "Did you know there's a new girl staying at the hotel? She looks like a cover model."

"I met her on the train. Her name is Giselle Campbell. She moved here with her father, Jack, who bought the Northern Lights Lodge," Alicia explained. "Laurel is her aunt."

"Think she'll join our youth choir?" Eli asked in an awestruck voice. "We could use some more girls, especially ones who look like her."

"You could always ask her." She picked up her purse.

"Alicia?"

"Yes?" She studied the boy, noting the change of tone in his voice.

"When's your next haircutting day? I think it's time for me to spruce up," Eli said.

"Soon." She hid her smile as she slid the strap of her bag over one shoulder. Clearly Eli wanted to make an impression on the newcomer. She turned around to leave but had to stop suddenly because Jack stood in front of her. "Oh, hello. Again."

"Hi." His gaze moved from her to Eli and back. "You do haircutting?"

"Only for the boys at Lives, and only if they want me to," she said, slightly embarrassed by his intense scrutiny. "A friend of mine in Vancouver taught me the basics. She's a hairdresser and runs a homeless shelter. She gives haircuts to anyone who wants one.

I don't have my license, but since a hairdresser only comes to Churchill every three or four months, I help out if someone asks. Laurel asked."

"I see." Were those piercing blue eyes more intense?

"Can I help you?" she asked when the silence stretched out too long.

"You're busy." Jack was acting very odd, as if he had something on his mind but was afraid to say it.

"Just going for groceries," Alicia explained. "Oh, this is Eli Long. He works for me. Eli, this is Mr. Campbell, from the lodge. Laurel's brother and Giselle's father," she added.

"Hi." Eli waved to Jack, then, as if he too sensed Jack's tension, got to work.

"Do you need something?" Alicia asked again.

"Maybe," Jack muttered. He shuffled his amazing shoes then looked at her. "Yes, please," he said in a firm voice. "I need your help."

"Sure." Alicia nodded. "With what?"

"With whom," he corrected. His gaze slid to Eli. "Giselle. I, er, did something—"

"Why don't we walk while you tell me?" she said, realizing that he didn't want to speak in front of Eli. She stepped outside and pulled the door closed behind them. As Jack walked beside her down the street, her pulse began to thrum at his closeness. "Well?"

"How about I treat you to coffee?"

"If you add a doughnut, I'll agree," she teased.

But Jack didn't smile. He simply nodded and began walking toward Common Grounds, a coffee shop down the street from Alicia's store. Sensing he needed a few moments to collect his thoughts, she caught up, saying nothing until they were seated with their coffee and doughnuts in front of them.

Jack's silence unsettled her. She needed to get him talking. A quick glance at the clock told her she'd need to hurry him a bit. Today was early closing at the Northern Store because of inventory taking. Grocery shopping and a decent dinner might have to wait till tomorrow.

Finally, without looking up at her, Jack spoke. "Giselle's run away."

Chapter Four

Jack felt like a fool.

He'd been a father for eleven years, yet the small, dark-haired beauty who had called him dad until recently still had the ability to tie him in knots. He saw Alicia struggling not to smile and glared at her.

"It's not funny."

"It kind of is," she said. "This is Churchill, Jack. There's no place to run. Unless she got on the train before it left?" Her smile faded as she studied him with concern.

"No, the train left before our big blowup," he told her.

"Then she's around town somewhere."

"She's on her way to Laurel's, and she says she's not coming back." He raked a hand through his hair, feeling helpless and a bit foolish. "I can't have her living out there, Alicia. There are six boys there. I don't care how sweet my sister says they are. My daughter is not staying at Lives with them. Anyway, even if I'd allow it, there's no room." He groaned. "This is a nightmare."

"Hardly." Alicia leaned back in her chair and studied him. "What was the argument about?"

"Her room." He couldn't look at her, wouldn't let her see how much Giselle's rejection of his surprise hurt.

"Her bedroom?" Alicia's dark eyebrows lifted. "What's wrong with it?"

"According to her, everything." Jack shrugged helplessly. "I had it professionally decorated as a surprise. I wanted to make it feel like home." He gave in to defeat. "Giselle hates it. She says I'm treating her like an infant, acts like I deliberately tried to offend her. I was trying to show how much I love her, how much I want her to be happy here."

Alicia studied him with that dark impenetrable stare for so long that frustration nipped at him. He should never have listened to Laurel's suggestion that he ask for Alicia's help. He accepted that his sister couldn't rush to his rescue. Besides, he wanted her there to meet Giselle when she arrived. But he suspected this was the first of Laurel's attempts at matchmaking.

"Never mind," he said, pushing his chair back and rising. "I shouldn't have bothered you. I'll figure out something." *Like what?* his brain demanded. *You can't even figure out what the issue is with Giselle.* Ignoring the inner voice, he turned to leave.

"I think you have the right idea." Alicia rose, asked the server for two take-out cups and a paper bag for their doughnuts.

"What are you doing?" Females. Jack had never felt more at a loss.

"Going with you to the scene of the crime. Maybe if I see the room, I can understand Giselle's anger. At the moment I'm at a total loss." Alicia held the cups and the bag. "Shall we?" she asked.

"I guess." Jack took the cups from her and followed her out of the café.

When they reached his hotel he led her inside, wondering why he held his breath as she studied the lobby where workmen were putting together the finishing touches. Was her approval so important?

"It's lovely, Jack. Rustic but not overdone. Very comfortable. Homey. Your guests will enjoy this." She smiled at him as she slid her fingertips over the rough stone of the fireplace.

"I used the same interior designer for Giselle's room," he complained.

"Maybe girls' bedrooms aren't her forte," Alicia murmured. "But hotel lobbies certainly are. Which way?"

"Follow me." Jack led the way to their private quarters, set their take-out cups down on a hall table, then opened the door to Giselle's room. When Alicia didn't immediately comment, he turned to study her.

His heart sank as Alicia's mouth formed a perfect *O*.

"What?" Jack shifted uncomfortably. All he could see was sweetness and love for his baby girl. What was so terrible about that?

"Oh, dear." Alicia set down the bag with the doughnuts, grabbed one of the cups and sank into a puffy pink chair inside the bedroom door. After another moment of looking around she took a long drink and sighed. "Oh, my."

"Will you stop saying that and tell me what I did wrong?" Jack bellowed. "Sorry," he said when he realized the harshness of his tone. "I didn't mean to bark at you, but what's wrong with this?"

"Where to start?" Alicia leaned back in the chair. "It's so…pink."

"Giselle's a girl," he said in his own defense. "And she likes pink."

"So do I. At least I used to." Alicia took another drink.

"Say what you need to," he growled, knowing he wouldn't like it.

"It's—it's like a pink fuzzy nest, for a baby chick or a bunny," she sputtered, then leaned back, as if she was afraid he'd explode.

And Jack felt like it. All the time he'd wasted, all

the work, all the money—none of which mattered a whit if his daughter hated being here.

He'd failed her. The lump in his throat grew.

"These stuffed toys." Alicia flicked a finger over the bunnies and elephants and giraffes.

"Giselle likes stuffed toys," he defended.

"Yes, but the floor, the bedspread, the lamp, the ceiling light—" She cleared her throat. "It's a room for a very young girl, Jack," she said quietly. "I doubt it's the kind of room a girl Giselle's age dreams of and I'm guessing that's what you want."

"It's a lot like her room was in Vancouver." Jack hated being on the defensive. He'd done this because of Giselle's complaints about having to relocate to a new, unfamiliar room in Churchill. How had he got it so wrong? "You mean she wants something more grown-up?"

"In my humble opinion, yes." Alicia looked relieved that he understood. "Did you tell your designer Giselle's age?"

"I can't remember." He frowned, trying to recall. "There were so many details with the hotel, so many things I never even thought of. I'm clueless about hotel management, but Laurel convinced me I could run this place with Teddy's instruction." He closed his eyes, pushed away the irritation and frustration and thought about it. "I think I said I wanted a special room for my little girl." He glanced around. "I guess that's what I got."

"You did. But Giselle isn't a little girl anymore." Alicia's gentle voice soothed his hurt feelings. "Part of the process of losing her mom has pushed Giselle to grow up. She's trying to figure out how to become an adult."

"And this room can't help her do that?" Deflated, he scanned the fripperies he'd been so sure Giselle would love.

"Let's just say it's not an almost-teen room." He could hear how carefully she chose her words and appreciated her gentleness.

"Okay." Jack let go of his disappointment. "How do I get it that way? Because my daughter is not going to live at Lives Under Construction."

"You want my help?" Alicia's brown eyes widened. Jack nodded, his brain noting in passing how pretty she was. She glanced around, then swiveled her gaze back to him. "This might hurt."

Did she think he was a wimp?

"I'm tough," he said, straightening his spine. "Go for it."

Jack kept his face stoic when she asked him to fetch two garbage bags. He remained resolute when she loaded all but two of the soft velvet toys and stuffed animals into the bags. He didn't even wince when Alicia carefully removed the frilly lace-edged lamps or asked his help to get down the flouncy curtains that blocked the view of Hudson Bay. But when she lifted the ruffled pink spread from the bed, he choked.

"That cost a fortune," he muttered.

Alicia simply raised one eyebrow.

"Go ahead," he groaned, holding the bag while she stuffed it inside. The room looked bare and unwelcoming. "Now what?" he demanded.

"Can I look around your lodge?" Alicia caught her long glossy hair in her hand and twisted it into some kind of knot on her head. She pinned it in place, then said thoughtfully, "There may be some things that we could use to help this room. Otherwise, you'll have to order stuff in and that could take days."

He didn't have days. He wanted his daughter home where he could keep her safe.

"Take whatever you need," Jack told her. He followed her through the hotel. A picture of wildflowers by a local artist graced the area behind the front desk. "Giselle helped me pick that out. She's got a thing about wildflowers." His heart took a dive as Alicia studied the painting, then looked at him. "You want that for her room. What do I put in its place?"

"Something else," she said quietly. Her gaze met his unflinchingly. This was not a woman who gave up easily. Actually, Jack appreciated that.

And so it went. Alicia ordered all the pink furniture removed from the room. She chose an armoire from a guest suite to house Giselle's television, and bedside lamps from his room.

"But I picked those out specially," he argued.

"For your daughter," Alicia reminded him. She raised one eyebrow. "Right?"

What could he do but nod to one of the workers who followed, collecting whatever Alicia chose? Jack's estimation of her abilities rose with every choice she made. A mirror and a silvery gray padded headboard drew everything together—fresh, young, not at all babyish.

The final result stunned him. Alicia had managed to capture Giselle's essence and she'd only just met his daughter. Jack looked at her in awe. He'd never guess this quiet, almost solemn woman who'd sat beside him on the train had so much insight.

"What goes there?" He pointed to the only bare wall in the room, hoping she had a solution. The pink walls now seemed like nothing more than a canvas to showcase all the new furnishings. Except for that wall. If left the way it was, Jack had a feeling Giselle wouldn't accept the room.

"You said she likes wildflowers?" Alicia asked, tapping a finger against her bottom lip as she studied him.

"She collects pictures of them." A sense of relief filled him. How was it he *knew* this amazing woman would find a solution?

"You'll suspect I did all this to sell you something," she warned. "But I have three perfect watercolors of local wildflowers in my store—one of white mountain avens, one of purple paintbrush and one of local orchids."

"Orchids? Here?" Jack suspected she was joking, but Alicia didn't smile.

"Yes, here, though they rely on special fungi on the ground instead of growing in trees like in the tropics. The only thing is the paintings aren't framed. I wonder…" She wasted only a moment before stepping into the hallway and motioning for him to follow. "Can we use those frames?" she asked, indicating an arrangement on the wall.

His beautiful lodge looked as if it had been ransacked. But if Jack had to choose between it and Giselle there was no contest. Still…

"We couldn't buy some frames locally?"

"That kind of thing is shipped in," she said. "Takes time."

Jack gave in. "Go get your watercolors while I take those down."

"I'll be right back." Alicia grinned. "You're such a *dad*," she teased, smiling at him.

She left and Jack sat down on the poofy chair, which now looked absolutely perfect with its pale green throw. He let his eyes wander through the room. It was perfect for Giselle. His gaze rested on the black desk beneath the window that waited for her to spread out her homework. His girl loved black furniture. He'd refused to buy it before, but somehow Alicia had made it an integral part of this retreat.

How had she known? Was it a female thing or did she have some knowledge of young girls? Who was Alicia Featherstone? Jack's brain hummed with questions. She was so different from the career women he'd known in Vancouver. He definitely wanted to know more about her.

Alicia burst into the room, breathless, with Eli trailing her, carrying the art.

"I brought along a couple of other things I thought might help give a Northern flavor. You don't have to keep them if you don't want." Alicia set a sculpture on the bedside table. "This brown bear is made completely of acorn husks applied to wood with local seeds."

"Giselle will love it. It looks like intricate work." He scanned the attached card, which told about the significance of brown bears in Native culture.

"This is a soapstone carving of a seal, a polar bear's idea of a gourmet dinner." She set it on the desk. "And this is a wampum belt. The Cree once used these to record family events. Giselle seemed quite interested in Native culture. I thought she could make the belt tell her story." She laid it over the back of the desk chair.

Amazed that Alicia had considered such detail, Jack could only watch as Eli framed the watercolors and hung them on the wall.

"Somehow this room looks exactly like her," Jack said with satisfaction when Alicia set the hot-pink phone on the desk. "I think Giselle will like this. A lot."

"I hope so." Alicia waved a hand as Eli left to return to the store. "I hope I haven't ruined your hotel. And if she doesn't like it, I'm happy to take back my stuff. I just—"

Was she nervous?

"Alicia." Jack reached out and smoothed the furrow on her forehead, marveling that she already felt like a good friend. At least she would have felt like that if she hadn't jerked back from his touch. He pretended not to notice. "I don't know how you did it, but my daughter is going to be ecstatic over this room. I can't thank you enough."

She looked at him a long time before the worry faded from her eyes and the twinkle returned. She chuckled.

"Be warned. When we get going on the sod house, you'll probably wish you'd never asked for my help."

If this room got his girl back home, Jack doubted he'd ever regret asking Alicia anything. Alicia Featherstone was a wonder woman.

He felt bemused by the many facets of this amazing woman. Business owner, haircutter, room decorator. He could hardly wait to find out what else Alicia could do. Her Native beauty was refreshing and stunning yet she seemed totally unaware of it. That intrigued him.

Though his brain sent up a warning, Jack ignored

it. Friendship wasn't off-limits and he had a hunch Alicia could become a good friend.

More than that he would not allow.

"I'm glad you could join us for dinner, Alicia," Laurel said as she took a seat beside her. "You know you're always welcome at Lives."

"Thanks. I'm glad, too," Alicia told her with a grin. "I didn't have time to get to the grocery store so my fridge is bare. This is way better than anything I'd make." She smiled at Giselle, who'd been watching her closely ever since she and Jack had arrived with Eli.

"I'll say grace and then we can eat." Laurel began to pray.

During the meal, Alicia was glad for the busy chatter of the boys talking about their day. That took away some of her nervousness about sitting next to Jack. With Giselle glaring at her dad and Jack mostly silent, there was an underlying tension in the room, but only to those in the know. Otherwise, it felt just like a family meal. Kids laughing, talking—she'd always wanted that at her dinner table.

"It's getting warmer and lighter every day, Alicia." Eli's gray eyes glowed. "We should be able to start on the sod house soon." He was part Cree and anything to do with his mother's culture intrigued him, which was why he'd asked to work in Alicia's store.

"Do you have a start date, Alicia?" Laurel rose

to get some more juice. "Who do you have lined up to help you?"

Alicia couldn't read her face, but she heard a hint underlying the woman's words that made her glance at Jack. He, too, stared at Laurel.

"Pastor Rick will help. He helps with everything around Churchill," Matt, the oldest of the boys, said.

"Yeah, and Kyle, though having him bring his new baby around the job site would be weird." Rod, one of the first boys to come to the program, snickered. "Being a new dad has him tied in knots."

Adam, Garret and Bennie were new to Lives and eager to hear more details.

"Jack has agreed to help us, too." Alicia thought Laurel's smile bloomed a little too widely. "He's going to get more information from the library for us," she continued uneasily. "We also have to wait for town council to determine which land they'll donate for us to build on. They're taking their time."

"So when can we start?" Rod pressed.

"If everything comes together, I plan on starting right after you guys finish school," Alicia told them. "If that works for you, Jack," she added.

The hotelier shrugged. "Should be okay."

"Great." He could have shown some enthusiasm, Alicia thought. She faced the boys. "Make sure you study hard. I don't want anyone to have to miss the fun because of summer school."

"You have summer school here, too?" Giselle asked in surprise.

The boys outdid each other trying to explain that their school was just like any other, and they made it clear that they intended to avoid summer school at all costs. Alicia chuckled, smothering her laughter when Jack's frown deepened into a glower because Eli smiled at Giselle and she smiled back.

"See? She's not your baby anymore," Alicia murmured.

Jack did not appreciate her humor. When the meal was over and the kitchen restored to order, he turned to Giselle. "We need to go home now," he said in a flat tone.

"I told you, I won't stay in that room." Giselle crossed her arms over her chest, her face frozen in a glare of mutiny. "It's like a playpen."

No doubt sensing tension, Laurel ushered the boys out of the room. Alicia tried to leave, too, but Jack's hand on her arm stopped her.

"Please wait," he said.

Alicia jerked away then nodded.

"Sorry." Jack gave her an odd look then turned to his daughter. "You may not stay here, Giselle. Your aunt doesn't have any extra room." Jack endured her icy glare with no reaction. Alicia applauded his fortitude. Lesser men would have weakened.

"It's time to go home," he said quietly.

"Home?" Scorn laced his daughter's voice.

"Yes. The lodge is our home now," he said with firmness. "I have something I want to show you, honey," he added in a softer tone.

"I don't think I want another surprise today." Despite her bravado, Giselle's bottom lip trembled.

Jack wrapped an arm around her shoulder and hugged her to his side.

"Give it a chance, please?" He lifted her chin. "I know your life right now isn't what you thought, but it doesn't have to be all bad."

Alicia's heart ached for the bereft twosome. Giselle wanted, needed her mom. Jack was doing everything he could to make her transition easier. She admired him for that. Silently she whispered a prayer for them while her brain cheered, *Come on, Giselle. He loves you so much. Give a little.*

"Please?" Jack murmured after pressing a kiss against her hair.

Giselle inhaled, then nodded. "Okay."

"Excellent." Jack beamed. He lifted her in the air and whirled her in a circle, as he'd probably done ever since she was little. "I love you, sweet pea."

"I love you, too." When he set her down, Giselle leaned back to study him. "But I still want you to find out who my birth parents are."

Giselle might be adopted, but in the girl's dark eyes Alicia saw the same dogged implacability as her father showed.

Jack remained silent. His gaze swung to Alicia.

She smiled, trying to mentally encourage him. He glanced back at his daughter.

"Okay, I'll make some more inquiries," he said at last. "But you—"

"I know. I won't get my hopes up. I'll try to be patient and I'll try not to be disappointed if things don't turn out as I hope." She straightened her shoulders. "I'm ready."

"Good." He shepherded them out to the car.

Alicia felt like a fifth wheel, but since she had no other way to get home, she got in the car, in the front seat beside Jack because Giselle insisted.

"Where'd you get this car?" she asked. "I don't think I've seen it around town before."

"You haven't. I had it shipped in," Jack said, his face closing up.

"It was my mom's car," Giselle murmured.

"Oh." Now Alicia really felt in the way. She waited until they reached town before she spoke. "You can drop me off here," she said. "I'll walk the rest of the way."

"No. You have to come." Jack flicked a look to the backseat. "Alicia and I have a surprise for you, honey."

"You and *Alicia?*" Giselle frowned.

"Well, I guess it's mostly Alicia's surprise." Jack pulled up beside his hotel, got out and came around to open Alicia's door. "Come on. Let's show her."

"I'm not very good with surprises," Giselle said. Her face reddened. "I guess you already know that."

"I'm not sure—" Alicia wanted to escape. But Jack gazed at her, a plea in his eyes. When a man looked at you like that, what could you do?

"Come on, Giselle," she said, twining her arm with the girl's. "Let's go look."

Jack led the way into the hotel. He paused in front of her bedroom door.

"This is for you. Because I love you. With Alicia's help." He pushed open the door.

Giselle's face transformed from dread to wonder. She gave a squeal then rushed inside, bounding from one thing to another.

Relieved, Alicia turned to smile at Jack.

"I guess she thinks it's okay," she murmured.

Thank you, he mouthed.

Such a silly thing, but her heart thrummed with delight.

"It's perfect. I can't wait to have a sleepover." Giselle danced from one foot to the other.

"A *girls'* sleepover," Jack added.

Alicia looked at Giselle and they groaned together. Giselle hugged her.

"How did you know my favorite color is green?" she asked.

"This." Alicia pointed to the tiny emerald ring on her pinkie finger. "And this." She touched a green clip in Giselle's hair. "And this." Her fingers brushed the green scarf looped around her neck.

"Daddy gave them to me." Giselle tipped her head to one side. "How did you know to do all this? Are you a designer or something?"

"Nothing like that." Alicia snuck a look at Jack and let out a pent up breath. He was smiling. "I just thought about what I'd like if I were your age and had a room like this."

"Good thinking." Giselle wrapped her arm around her father's waist and looked at him adoringly. "It's absolutely perfect, isn't it, Daddy?"

Daddy. The two of them are a family.

She stood there, watching father and daughter bond, deeply touched by their precious reuniting. Her part had been small, but a tiny thrill coursed through Alicia that she'd been able to help bring them together, to re-create the bond that joined them.

If only she had someone to cling to, someone to love. As she watched Giselle and Jack, the ache in her heart grew. Because of *him* she had no family. Because of him she was missing everything about her son. *He'd* ruined her life.

Though a silent prayer helped suppress her pain, it didn't stop her heart from constricting or her throat from closing with emotion. All she could think about was escaping before they noticed and she spoiled their reunion.

"I have to go," she said, and wheeled toward the door.

"Alicia?" Giselle called. Alicia half turned to face her. "Thank you very much for helping my dad with this. I appreciate it a lot." Her thin arms wrapped around Alicia's neck, enveloping her in another hug.

"Welcome to Churchill. I think you and your father are going to love it here." For a moment Alicia hugged her back. Then she eased herself free and hurried away. She thought she heard Jack call her name, but she ignored it and kept walking, desperate to be alone, to get away from the cloying constriction of emotions that returned whenever she remembered that day and all she'd lost.

Once in her apartment, Alicia sat in front of her electric fireplace, craving the heat it gave off. Though it had felt warm outside earlier, her soul was icy cold, her spirit crushed, her heart broken.

It was *his* fault Alicia hadn't realized the implications that would follow from giving her child to another. Never to hear *Mom,* never to be hugged, never to know the soft touch of a child's lips against her skin. Giselle's embrace forced her to realize she'd given all that away.

Alicia had been trying to do the right thing, but somehow, until now, she'd never fully appreciated all that Mr. Parcet's actions had cost her. Not until she'd seen Jack and Giselle strengthening the bonds that held their family together.

I'm so alone, her heart whispered. *There's no one to love me, to care for me.* She thought of her son, growing up, changing, learning to love.

Will I ever know his voice or hear him laugh? Does he have a family who loves him, a mother who will give him what I couldn't? Will I ever have a family, a child to love? Will I ever be loved?

It took until twilight faded into the blackness of midnight before the Father's love soothed her bruised heart, before she could finally let go.

"It doesn't matter about me, God," she whispered. "Just keep my child safe from Mr. Parcet."

Alicia thought of Jack, his big strong arms wrapped around his little girl, protecting her from anything that could hurt her.

Give my boy a dad like Jack who will protect him, she prayed.

But when morning came, Alicia knew it wasn't just enough to pray about it. She had to do whatever she could to protect her child and that meant revealing one of her secrets. She picked up the phone.

"Laurel, how do I go about finding my former social worker?"

Chapter Five

"I've made a few calls about Mrs. Endersley, Alicia," Laurel said into the phone. "Give me a few days to get some responses. Then you can go from there. Meanwhile, I'm glad you trusted me with your secret. I promise I won't tell anyone."

Jack leaned against the door frame of Lives' kitchen and waited until his sister had hung up. "What secret?"

"Jack!" Laurel jumped, then put a hand to her chest. "You always did try to sneak up on me."

"Not sneaking," he said. "Just waiting till you'd finished. What secret?"

"If I told you, I'd be breaking my promise and I don't break promises. Ever." She gave him a coy smile. "Your suspicious policeman's mind doesn't have to worry about Alicia. She's the salt of the earth. She helped you out, didn't she?"

"A lot," he admitted with a nod. For the past week

he hadn't been able to stop thanking Alicia for her decorating assistance. But neither could he stop the niggling feeling that happened when his instincts issued a warning. Like they were doing now. "I know almost nothing about her. What can you tell me?"

"That she's sincere. That she's honest." Laurel shrugged.

"Does she have family?" Jack pressed, trying to satisfy his need to know more about this woman he couldn't stop thinking about. "I know she said her parents died in a plane crash, but…"

"Jack, what's wrong?" Laurel frowned. He knew then that he couldn't evade her questions.

"Ever since that night in Giselle's room, it seems like she's avoiding me. It's odd." His uneasiness wouldn't let up, but he didn't appreciate his sister's scrutiny. "It's not for me, it's for Giselle. You know how I always vet everyone my daughter hangs around with. Giselle's been spending a lot of time at Alicia's store. I just want to know more about the woman."

"Uh-huh." Laurel gave him her implacable stare.

"Actually I've had second thoughts about working with her on that sod house."

"Oh, why?" she demanded. "Because you don't know her well enough?"

"Because there's something odd about her project." Jack gave vent to his frustration. "Far as I can tell, Alicia has no building plans, in fact, no real information about what this house should look like. Except in her head."

"So?" Laurel's blasé expression annoyed him.

"She's done no prep work." He tried to explain his concerns. "We've a little over a month until she claims to want to start, but what's the plan? What are we going to do first?"

"Alicia knows what she's doing, Jack. She always does with these projects." Laurel laughed. "You're a perfectionist. You like every *i* dotted and *t* crossed ahead of time. Not all of us work that way. Maybe she has some information coming. You could always ask her about it, couldn't you?" she asked with a hint to her voice.

"I could," he agreed. "If she'd stop avoiding me."

"Why would she be avoiding you?" Laurel's blue eyes narrowed. "Did something happen between you?"

"Not the way I think you mean." Jack raked a hand through his hair. "That night, when we took Giselle back to see her room, everything seemed fine. Alicia was smiling, enjoying Giselle's reaction. Then it was like she shut down. Suddenly her face went blank. Before I could ask what happened, she'd left. Since then, every time we meet she's in a hurry or makes some excuse to leave."

"So she's busy." Laurel held up the coffeepot to ask if he wanted some, put it down when he refused.

"Maybe you should take her out for dinner and ask her about it." She shot him a wink.

He glared at her. "I told you, I'm not going to get involved again."

"Then shouldn't you be glad she's avoiding you?" Laurel smirked.

"Maybe, but I'm worried that this avoidance thing is some kind of game." His sister might have been widowed years ago, but she believed everyone else needed romance in their lives, especially him.

"Game? Alicia?" His sister shook her head with a vehemence that surprised him. "No way."

"It could be. Maybe she's playing hard to get or something." He felt like an idiot when his sister burst out laughing. "You don't see that?"

"Not in the least. If anything, Alicia would run the other way. Maybe she is," Laurel said thoughtfully. "Maybe she thought you asked too much and now she's trying to distance herself."

Jack thought about it and discarded the notion while Laurel sipped her coffee.

"Listen, Jack. In all the time I've known Alicia, she's never been involved with anyone. She's friendly and straightforward, but she's always been a loner. I think you have this wrong."

"I hope so," Jack told her, "because I'm just not interested in Alicia Featherstone."

"The feeling is entirely mutual."

Jack whirled around, almost groaning at the sight of Alicia standing in the doorway.

"I didn't mean that the way it sounded," he said.

"I did." Alicia's hands clenched on the woven bag she held. "I don't do relationships. I'll take all the friendships I can get, but I am not romantically interested in you, Jack. So you can relax. And I'd really appreciate it if you'd stop asking everyone in town about me. If you want to know something, ask *me*."

Her words should have relieved his worry that she was looking for a more personal relationship with him. Instead Jack was intrigued by the raspy way she spoke, the deep emotion that filled her voice and the way her fingertips whitened as she gripped her handbag. If she wasn't interested, why was Alicia so defensive?

"I'm sorry," he apologized. "I didn't mean to offend you."

Alicia didn't answer. Instead, she drew in a deep breath, as if she needed fortification.

"You're usually very busy at Tansi on Saturdays," Laurel said, breaking the tension in the room. "What brings you all the way out here this late in the day?"

"They told me at the hotel that Jack was here." She lifted her head and faced him head-on, defiance in her eyes. "I need to speak to you. About Giselle."

If this was some kind of game, he didn't get it. He'd worried she might try to initiate something between them, but he hadn't expected she'd use Giselle to do it. And yet, that didn't make sense given her body language.

"Excuse me. I'll leave you two to talk." Laurel walked out.

"What about Giselle?" he asked.

"She stole something from my store. I want it back. If I have to, I'll go to the police."

Jack stared.

If Alicia Featherstone was trying to build a relationship with him, she had the oddest method of going about it.

"Giselle—steal?" He shook his head. "I don't believe you."

"I can hardly believe it myself." Alicia's dignified tone surprised him. Clearly she'd had her word questioned before. When? he wondered. "Unfortunately, I saw her."

Incredulous, Jack sank onto a chair, unable to believe what he was hearing. He'd thought, hoped, this move to Churchill would be a new start for Giselle and him. But if Alicia was telling the truth, everything that *could* go wrong *was* going wrong.

For the first time in his life Jack had no idea how to fix things. But he had a hunch it was going to involve working with Alicia Featherstone. Oddly enough, he was pretty sure that keeping this lovely woman at arm's length was going to be much harder than he'd previously thought, especially since his questions about her kept mounting.

* * *

"I'm so sorry, Giselle." Alicia stared at the scrap of paper she'd picked up off the register. "I didn't see your note. I only saw you take the box. When I called, you didn't answer. In fact, you ran faster. I tried to think of a reason for your actions, but when I didn't hear from you— I'm terribly sorry."

A glance at Jack's face told her that her apology wasn't enough. He'd been rigid and unsmiling ever since he'd walked into her shop with his daughter.

"I'd never steal from you," Giselle said in a hurt tone. "I stuck that note on top of the register to explain. How could you miss it?"

"I don't know." Alicia stared at the paper in her hand. She recognized the carefully printed letters of her name, but what was written inside the note was a mystery to her. But she could hardly say that.

"What *did* you see?" Giselle asked.

"I was halfway down the stairs when I heard a noise. I saw you grab the box. It took me a minute to regroup but by then you were rushing out the door. As I said, I ran after you and called but you didn't respond. You just kept running." She exhaled. "I figured you were running away, that you'd stolen the box."

She hated saying this, hated the look on Jack's face and hated that she'd made him so defensive. Best to get the whole story out and hope he'd understand.

"I locked up and went to the hotel to talk to you,

but no one knew where you were. They sent me to your father at Laurel's."

"I didn't hear you call me," Giselle told her. "When I came in here I called you a couple of times. You didn't answer so I scribbled that note to explain."

"But why did you take the box?" Alicia asked.

"A guest at our hotel, Mr. Fraser, begged me to pick up a memento for his wife right before the train left," Giselle explained. "I didn't have much time. That's why I was hurrying. I'd seen the box yesterday when I stopped by. I knew it would be perfect to hold her earrings. She has beautiful earrings."

"I see." Alicia's cheeks burned with shame, even more so with Jack's blue eyes fixed on her.

"I tried to get back in time but you'd gone. He gave me this." Giselle tugged a wad of cash from her jeans pocket and laid it on the counter as if it burned her hands. "There's more than enough to pay for the box. He said to keep the extra money for a tip, but I don't want it now."

"But you must take it," Alicia exclaimed. "You went to so much trouble for him." She stared at the money, nibbling her lip as she wondered how to handle this. She could add, that wasn't the problem. But with Jack hanging over her, making her nervous, she'd probably fumble and that would be so embarrassing. "I, uh, can't remember how much we had the box priced at."

"I kept the tag." Giselle pulled out the little ticket and smoothed it on the counter. "Go ahead. Count it. It's all there."

Alicia was determined not to look as if she didn't trust the girl.

"I believe you, Giselle." Alicia smiled at her. "And I'm sorry I misjudged you. I appreciate you selling the box and I insist that you take your tip. I already feel bad enough."

"Are you sure?" Giselle frowned.

"I'm positive. I'm so sorry, Giselle. It's just that I've lost several valuable pieces this year and…" Alicia stopped, knowing her justification wasn't helping. Jack's scowl remained. "I apologize again, Giselle. I'm really sorry."

"Apology accepted." Giselle grinned, counted out the sale price, which she pushed toward Alicia, and tucked away her tip money. "If I was in charge of looking after all these lovely things, I guess I'd be protective, too," she said.

"That's very kind of you." Alicia returned her smile. How could she have thought Giselle was spoiled? She was really very sweet.

"This is the most fascinating place, isn't it, Daddy?" Giselle continued. "Do we have time for me to look around? Alicia's rearranged that corner. I never noticed those things last time I was here."

"Please look all you want. Everything there is half price." She waited until Giselle had wandered off toward the footwear that was left over from last year. Then she scooped the cash into the register, fully conscious that Jack's glaring gaze never left her.

"I'm so sorry, Jack."

"I knew my daughter wouldn't steal," he said in a stiff tone.

"I didn't want to believe she would have, either, but look at my side of it. When she didn't return with the box or pay for it, I couldn't figure out any other explanation. I truly am sorry, Jack." Alicia didn't know what else to say. There was nothing that would make her mistake look better.

"Giselle said she came back here to give you the money as soon as the train was gone, but you were already locked up." Jack's narrowed gaze demanded an explanation.

"I went with someone to deliver meals-on-wheels." Alicia wasn't going to make any more excuses. She could only apologize again and hope he'd forgive her.

If only she could read properly, this wouldn't have happened. She had seen the note with her name but assumed it was from a client. She'd been going to ask Eli about it on Monday. But there was nothing to tell her that slip of paper wasn't like a lot of the others that came through her shop.

It was her own fault, of course. She was too stubborn to go to the school and ask someone to tutor her. She was also afraid. If certain people in town knew she couldn't read, they might think she wasn't a good risk at business, maybe even try to cancel her loan. Her business was all she had. Alicia couldn't, wouldn't jeopardize it. But it was clear now—she had to learn to read. Somehow.

"I thought you knew Giselle well enough to know she would never take anything without paying," Jack said quietly.

Alicia fiddled with some things on the counter, busywork to avoid looking at him. He was too silent and she worried he wouldn't be able to forgive her.

"I know that now," she said finally.

"But I realize that there could have been a problem." Jack spoke slowly, thoughtfully. "No business can afford to lose its merchandise. As owners we have to protect our investment." His tight expression eased. "If it's any consolation, I did reprimand Giselle for not phoning to leave a message."

"It wasn't her fault, Jack. It was mine. But thank you for understanding." She noticed the time. Her store should be closed by now, but since Jack and Giselle were still there, Alicia opened the box of handmade kites she'd received by post this morning. She needed something to keep her focus off him.

"What are those for?" He bent to look at the one she'd pulled from its package.

"I always get a stock of handmade kites for Canada Day," she explained. "We have a town-wide kite-flying contest which I sponsor."

"But this is only May," Jack said, his face incredulous. "July first is six weeks away."

"When you live up here, you have to be prepared. Last year I had to pay air freight to get them here on time. That cut my profit to almost nothing." She threaded tiny poles into the holes, but the effect wasn't quite right. "Hmm. These aren't the same as last year's."

"If all else fails, read the directions." Jack grinned at her, spread the sheet out on the counter and waited.

Alicia kept her head down, refusing to show the panic that gripped her.

"You read, I'll assemble," she said, then lifted her gaze. "Unless you have to get back to work?"

Half of her wished he had to go. The other half wanted him to stay, which was crazy. Ever since she'd been attacked, being near a man, any man, made her jittery. But it wasn't exactly nervous jitters she felt around Jack. So what was it?

"Don't tell me you've tucked your glasses away somewhere again," he teased.

"How'd you guess?" she asked, secretly relieved to have an excuse.

"Laurel does it all the time," Jack said. His eyes twinkled as if he'd caught her playing a trick. "She thinks I don't notice, but I do."

"That's not—" She stopped, seized the explanation he offered. "You see too much," she murmured.

"Alicia, there's no reason to be ashamed of bad eyesight." The kindness in his voice touched her.

"I'm not ashamed." But shame was exactly what she was feeling. Shame about deceiving him, among other things. "Okay, I am ashamed. And frustrated with myself if you must know. How I missed seeing that note…" She shook her head.

"It doesn't matter. People make mistakes." His hand brushed hers as he corrected the way she was threading the wood through the flaps on the back of the kite. "I shouldn't have jumped on you like that. Sorry."

"Please, can we forget it?" His touch did weird things to her stomach and made her nerves ripple, so Alicia let him take charge of the kite and backed up a little. "I guess I don't have to tell you I'm not good at assembling stuff."

"Lots of people aren't." In a few minutes, Jack had the kite put together. "There you go."

"Thank you." She admired it for a moment, loving the black eagle shape. "To a Cree, eagles mean strength, wisdom and bravery. I think this one will really soar over the cliffs." As she arranged the unassembled kites she glanced at him over one shoulder. "By the way, how's your business doing?"

"Thanks to Teddy, we're almost fully booked for the polar bear season," he said in a satisfied tone.

"Told you. Nobody knows more about being a hotelier than Teddy." She turned to ask if Giselle needed help, but the girl seemed enthralled by the beadwork on a pair of leather slippers and didn't answer. "Want a cup of coffee?" she asked Jack.

The words slipped out before Alicia realized that offering Jack coffee meant he'd hang around here longer. If she wasn't careful he might get too close and guess her secret. Still, when the sod house project went ahead, he'd be working with her. She could hardly ignore him.

"I'd love a coffee. I was up early this morning and never got my second cup." He sat down on the stool Alicia dragged out from the back room and accepted the coffee she offered a few minutes later. "Giselle's become fascinated with everything in this store. I knew she was curious about Native Canadians when she did that paper for her class, but it's developed into an obsession since we moved to Churchill. I hope she won't become a nuisance."

"I'm happy to have her stop by whenever she likes." Alicia grinned. "After all, my goal is to educate about my ancestry. Giselle is an apt pupil. And a great saleswoman," she said, deadpan.

He chuckled.

"She sure has a lot of questions," Alicia murmured.

"Tell me about it." He rolled his eyes. "She won't stop questioning me. Yesterday she asked me to help her make pemmican. I know it's a Native food but

I haven't a clue what's in it." Jack's face displayed his apprehension.

"The word pemmican comes from the Cree word, *pimîhkân*."

"Meaning?" Jack lifted one eyebrow.

"Fat or grease." Alicia giggled at his skeptical expression. "The specific ingredients used were whatever was available. The meat was often bison, moose, elk or deer and then they added fruits if they had them available, cranberries and saskatoon berries sometimes. If they could get them they'd also use cherries, currants, chokecherries and blueberries, but that was mostly for ceremonial and wedding pemmican."

"Sounds a little like those weird health food bars my wife used to eat." For a moment pain fluttered across his face, but then he grinned. "Except Simone wouldn't have been caught dead eating fat."

"Granola bars are a good comparison," Alicia said. "Europeans who came to Canada for the fur trade and many Arctic explorers adopted pemmican because it was a high-energy food they could easily carry."

"You see, Dad," Giselle said as she looked up from the display. "Alicia knows everything about this stuff."

"I didn't realize you were listening in." Alicia smiled at her. "You seem pretty keen on learning about my ancestors."

"Of course." Giselle shrugged. "I am Canadian. It's my history, too."

"Smart girl. I like your attitude." In truth, Alicia encountered very few people who learned about the original settlers in the land and then not only embraced that knowledge, but sought to learn more. Giselle was an eager pupil. "I don't know what your duties are at the hotel, but if you're interested, you're welcome to help us with some weekend events we hold throughout the summer."

"I'd love it!" Giselle twirled around, her face glowing with excitement. "But I hardly know anything. There's so much I need to learn."

"You could always visit the museum. It has lots of information and many examples of Native culture." Alicia chanced to glance Jack's way and noted the frown marring his good looks. "As long as it's okay with your father," she added.

"Daddy doesn't mind. He likes me to keep busy," Giselle assured her as she hugged Jack. "I can easily fit working here around my chores at the hotel. Right, Dad?"

"If you want," Jack said. It seemed to Alicia that he swallowed the rest of his coffee a little too quickly. Then he rose. "I'd better go. Teddy Stonechild is going to stop by tonight and show me how to update our reservation system to better use an online booking company. Thanks for the coffee."

"Thanks for your help with the kites." She smiled, half relieved that he was finally leaving. Maybe once those blue eyes were off her, her breathing would even out.

"Oh, I almost forgot." Jack drew a sheet of paper from his shirt pocket and held it out. "This is a list of resources the library is able to order in for the sod house. Why don't you take a look and check off the ones you think would be most helpful?"

"Uh, sure." Alicia couldn't do anything but take the paper from him. As usual when she was flustered, even the words she knew would turn to gibberish. Her stomach sank like a rock in the harbor.

"It wouldn't be a bad idea to order them right away," he continued, his eyes narrowed as he watched her. "That way we'd have lots of time to research so we know what we're doing."

"Good idea." She forced a smile then glanced sideways at Giselle. "Maybe you'd like to be part of this, too," she invited. As Alicia explained about the sod house, Giselle's brown eyes glowed with anticipation.

"I want to help, Daddy," she begged.

"Honey, it will be hard work. We have to dig in permafrost to get a foundation down. Manual labor," he said, only half teasing.

"I'm not useless. I can dig as well as Alicia or anyone else." A quiet dignity threaded through Giselle's voice. "I'm not a baby, Dad."

"I'm beginning to realize that." His gaze met Alicia's.

She had to look away as the connection between

them seemed to vibrate. Her reactions to Jack were strong but very different from those she experienced around other men. She didn't understand why just seeing him caused this odd nervousness.

"Technically, Tansi is closed so we'd better leave." He ruffled Giselle's hair. "You promised me you'd help with those housekeeping lists."

"Housekeeping." Giselle made a face. "How boring that will be after all these interesting things." She glanced over her shoulder then sighed. "Okay. I made a promise. I'll keep it. See you at church tomorrow, Alicia."

"Bye." Alicia waggled her fingers and watched father and daughter leave. With Jack gone the tenseness in her shoulders eased. But that lasted only a moment, until she looked down at the paper he'd given her. She turned the sheet right side up. Now what? She could hardly tell Jack she couldn't even read the titles let alone the books.

She was proud of her accomplishments. She'd made a life for herself, set up a business and ran it successfully, gradually paying off her loans. But in spite of all of that, she felt stupid. She was twenty-five and she couldn't even read a book.

Let alone figure out how to find her son.

I don't think I can do this on my own, God. I'll need help to find him. Please let Laurel find my former social worker.

Alicia had a lot of plans for her store, but now

they were all on hold. First she had to make sure her son was safe.

That was another thing she had to keep from Jack. So many secrets… But keeping them was worth it when there was so much was at stake. She'd given up her child to insure he had a future. Even though ten years had passed, his happiness was still her primary goal. Now she just had to find him without drawing anyone's suspicions.

Including the handsome former cop's.

"Alicia's really nice, isn't she, Dad?" Giselle draped herself on the floor in front of the fireplace in their private living room. "I really like her." She paused, then murmured, "But I feel like there's something wrong."

"Wrong?" Jack frowned. As far as he could tell, there was nothing wrong with the lovely woman. She had accused Giselle of stealing but she also kept coming to their rescue, most recently by offering his slightly bored daughter a job on the sod house. "With her business, you mean? Or because she accused you of stealing?"

"Technically, I guess I did steal," Giselle said thoughtfully. "I mean I did take something out of her store without paying for it." She nibbled on her bottom lip. "I think that scared her. I don't think Alicia has a lot of money, Daddy."

"Being self-employed is never easy," Jack agreed,

surprised by his child's mature consideration. "So is that what you meant about something being wrong?"

"No. Didn't you notice when you handed her that paper about the resource books?" Giselle prodded. "It was *upside down* and she didn't turn it right when she glanced at it, either. She just set it down."

"Maybe she was thinking about something else," he offered.

"Okay. But—" Giselle stared into the fire. "Then there are her glasses."

"Her glasses? Yeah, I noticed that, too." He frowned, puzzling over those missing glasses.

"She never seems to have them handy. If you needed glasses to see well, wouldn't you keep them nearby?" Her intent brown gaze rested on him, waiting.

She had a point. Jack waited for her to continue.

"I like Alicia so much. But sometimes I feel like she's hiding something." She let the words die away. "It's probably me. I'll figure it out and try to help if I can."

"I don't think there's anything wrong with Alicia, but it's very kind of you to try to help her, honey." A spurt of pride bubbled up inside him.

"It's what the Bible says we're supposed to do. 'Bear one another's burdens.'" Giselle grinned at him. "I'm sure Alicia could help you bear your burden—me."

The quotation made Jack shift uncomfortably.

Was Giselle reminding him he hadn't been to church in a very long time? Or did his daughter, spurred by her aunt, think he needed companionship? Whatever, it was time to make his position clear.

"Listen, I know you probably think things were better when your mom was alive, but we're still a family. I'm not looking to replace your mom, not that I could."

For the first time Jack couldn't immediately summon up Simone's face. He glanced at the photograph sitting on the fireplace mantel and felt like a traitor for needing that prod to recall the straight sculpted lines of her face, her glittering green eyes and the way her blond hair sprang back from her face.

"She was a very special woman."

"You always say that, but special can mean anything. What do you mean when you say it about Mom?" Giselle asked, her face resting in her palms, elbows on the area rug.

Jack groped for a way to explain. "Whenever she came in the room she was like sunshine that lights up all the dark corners. She was always smiling and happy. You must remember her laugh."

Giselle shook her head slowly, as if reluctant to admit it. "Sometimes I can hardly remember her at all," she said very softly. "Is that wrong?"

"No, not wrong." Jack felt ill equipped to have this conversation, but he had to reassure his child. "People we love are always in our hearts. The good times, the fun we had together, the love we shared, that's all tucked inside you. You won't forget your mom, Giselle. Not ever."

"I hope not," she agreed quietly. After a pause she asked, "I'm not really like her, am I?"

"Physically, you mean?" Jack asked.

"There's that—she was beautiful and glamorous, and I'm not. But in other ways, too. She liked quiet and peace. I like lots of people around." Giselle grimaced. "And I'm messy. Mom never had a hair out of place."

"Your mother was lovely. But you're pretty, too, honey," he assured her.

"She used to tell me about when she was growing up. She had so many friends." Giselle frowned. "I've never had more than one really close friend."

"Giselle, honey, just because you're different doesn't mean you aren't loved," he insisted. "Anyway, you're like her in your heart. Both of you are generous and kind."

"I'm not. I was mean to Alicia that first day on the train," Giselle admitted. "Mom liked to keep it secret when she did stuff. I remember her shushing me when I wanted to talk about the Christmas dinner she organized for the homeless shelter. Alicia's like that, I think."

Her reference to Alicia irritated him though he didn't know why.

"I would have bragged about what I did." Giselle

went silent, staring into the fire, lost in thought. Finally she asked, "Do you think Alicia has memories of happy family times like we do?"

"Probably. Why do you ask?" A twinge of frustration grew inside him. She constantly brought up Alicia's name, yet, from that first day they'd arrived Alicia had been there for her, helped fix her room, as a mother would. It was only natural Giselle thought about her.

But Jack now wondered if he'd been wrong to ask for Alicia's help. He'd been totally confounded by his daughter's reaction to his pink creation, but maybe he shouldn't have gone to Alicia. Maybe he'd encouraged Giselle to start thinking of Alicia as a maternal figure.

The maelstrom of questions roiling inside his head was disrupted by his daughter's thoughtful voice.

"Alicia always seems sad to me," Giselle mused aloud.

"She was smiling and laughing when we left her store."

"Yes, but I think that was for our benefit." Giselle nodded, her eyes narrowed. "I don't think she was smiling inside. She kept giving you these weird looks. Not puppy love stuff, Dad, so don't get all twisted. More like suspicious. Or worried. Kind of like she doesn't quite trust you."

"Really?" Jack raised one eyebrow, surprised only because Giselle was confirming what he'd felt.

"Maybe something else is bothering her, something she doesn't want to talk about." Giselle rose in one fluid motion.

"That's probably it," he agreed. He hadn't known Alicia long. It would be better to keep his distance until he did. "Are you sure you want to get so involved in the sod house?"

"I want to help. It's not organizing a Christmas dinner like Mom did, but it could be my contribution." She kissed his cheek, hugged him then hurried away, fingers flying over her phone. "Wait till Marni finds out," she called over one shoulder.

Marni had been Giselle's best friend since kindergarten, but Jack hoped his daughter would soon find a close friend here in Churchill. Maybe then she wouldn't want to spend so much time around Alicia Featherstone.

Like he did?

Jack struggled the rest of the evening, but failed to suppress thoughts of the lovely Native woman. He was already thinking about Alicia way too much. Would working together on the sod house intensify those thoughts? And if it did?

The thought tantalized him. To get closer to Alicia, to figure out why she was so reserved, so secretive—something inside him craved answers to his questions about her.

But as twilight lingered, he realized he couldn't give in to that need to know. He couldn't let himself care about her, though that would be easy. But going through the terrible loss as he had with Simone—no. Never again.

Friends, that's all he and Alicia could be.

Chapter Six

Jack perused the book's cover then added it to his growing "borrow" pile on the library table. One benefit to owning a hotel with only a train and air transport to bring guests was that on slack days he could grab a few moments on his deck with a book and a coffee or sit on the stony beach with the waves as background music for his reading. Escapism without leaving home when June nights stayed light well into the morning hours.

"Jack Campbell said you could order these for our sod house project, Barb."

Hearing his name, Jack peeked through the stacks. Alicia stood at the main desk, holding out a sheet of paper. She looked very businesslike in a royal-blue jacket over a white sweater and dark jeans. Her hair splayed over her shoulders in a straight fall of midnight-black. Her cheeks were rosy and her eyes sparkled with good health. Jack could hardly tear his eyes away.

"You're sure you want so many?" Barb, the librarian, asked in a surprised tone.

"Yes, please." Alicia smiled at her wide-eyed look. "We're not exactly sure which we'll need, so it's better to be prepared."

The librarian took the list and set it near her keyboard.

"Thanks very much. Give me a call when they come in, okay? Oh, by the way..." Alicia opened her bag and pulled out a foil-wrapped package. "Here's a loaf of that banana bread you said you liked. I made a fresh batch this morning."

"Before or after your run?" Barb grinned as she took the loaf, held it to her nose and inhaled with deep satisfaction.

"Before." Alicia winked. "I can't sleep when the sun's up."

"You never do. I'm glad you stopped by, and not only because of this lovely treat," Barb said. She reached under her desk and pulled out a small box. "The rest of your tapes came. They're on extended loan so you can keep them for three months."

"Excellent." Alicia tucked the package into her bag. "I don't know if that's long enough with summer coming and everything so busy, but I'm eager to get started."

"I can always ask for another extension." Barb

signed them out. "You're doing very well. I never made it through even the first level of French."

"I think the tapes make it easier," Alicia murmured.

Alicia was learning French? Again her multifaceted personality surprised Jack. His elbow hit the stack of books and sent one crashing to the floor. He quickly replaced it, knowing he'd been skulking behind the stacks long enough. Barb would think he was spying. He gathered up his novels and walked toward the counter.

"Hi Alicia," he said, surprised by the rush of excitement that hit him.

"Hi. That's a lot of books." She blinked when he set them all on the countertop. "Are you planning a reading holiday?"

"I wish." He chuckled, trying but utterly incapable of stemming his admiration for the way her glorious hair fell over her shoulders like a dark shawl. "I'm preparing for when I get a spare minute. I like to read."

"You must if you're checking out that many books." Alicia wore a funny look Jack couldn't quite interpret.

"I blew the budget on my e-reader during our seventeen-hour train ride from Thompson so I'm back to borrowing books," he explained.

"Oh," she said, her face blank for an instant before she glanced at Barb. "Well, I'd better go if I'm to have a coffee break before Eli takes off. Bye." She fluttered her fingers in a wave and walked out, her long, lean legs eating up the distance toward the beach.

"She really moves, doesn't she?" Barb stood staring after her. "I wish I could walk that fast."

"My sister told me you had a hip replacement not long ago. I don't think you're supposed to move quite that fast after major surgery." He watched Barb stamp each of his books. "Can I see the list of books Alicia gave you to order for the sod house project? I'm curious which she chose."

"She didn't *choose* any. She wants them all." Barb frowned. "Alicia's never ordered books from me before, only tapes." She shrugged. "In order to build the sod house, I guess she needs reference material."

So Alicia wasn't a reader. Jack mulled on that as he left the library. He dumped his books in the cab of the ratty old truck that had come with the hotel. As he turned, he noticed Alicia sitting on a bench on the beach, sipping from a thermal cup as she stared over the bay.

"Don't do it," he told himself, but that didn't stop his feet from crunching over the stones to where she sat. "Mind if I join you?" He couldn't quite hide his wince as the sharp pebbles pressed into his soles.

"I think you'd better sit before you fall down." Her gaze slid to his feet then back to his face. Her brown eyes glinted. "I warned you those boots wouldn't work here."

"They work perfectly at the hotel." He chuckled when the corner of her mouth lifted in a smile. He caught the tiniest hint of smugness before she resumed her scrutiny of the bay. "Am I bothering you?"

"No. I like to take a break here every day if I can manage it," she said. "I never get enough of watching the whales."

"They are amazing," he agreed, studying the big dark mammals as they arched and dipped in the sparkling water. "By the way, how did that internet site work out for you?"

She turned to study him, her forehead pleated. "Internet site?"

"About adoption. Remember, I gave you the address on the train?" Jack frowned when Alicia quickly slewed her eyes back to the water.

"Oh, that. I haven't gotten round to it yet." She sounded as if she was in no hurry.

"But I thought—" It was none of his business. Alicia had seemed eager to continue her search but maybe something had changed. "You look happy today."

"I am. When you look at all this—" She waved a hand to encompass the beach, the shore, the sky. "Doesn't it make you think of God's greatness?"

Like that, Jack's good mood dissipated.

"Actually," he said, his eyes on the grounded ship peeking out of the water, "when I see the *MV Ithaca* over there, grounded on this shoreline, where it's been since 1960, God's greatness isn't what comes to mind. He abandoned that ship and its crew here."

"An eighty-mile-an-hour gale and a broken right rudder caused the problem," she corrected quietly.

"A problem God could have prevented." Jack clamped his lips shut, determined to say no more. He'd vowed the day he arrived in Churchill not to rehash his resentment toward God anymore. Simone was dead. Neither his anger nor his bitterness would bring her back.

"You're angry at God," Alicia said quietly.

"I suppose you think that's terrible," he said, trying to stem the emotions he felt inside.

"I think it's perfectly normal." Alicia smiled gently. "I've been there myself. But it didn't help me much."

Jack frowned. "Meaning?"

"Well, stuff happens. I don't know why. You don't know why. But does it matter why?" She shrugged. "The important thing is what comes next."

"Next?" Jack felt he'd lost track of the conversation.

"The past happened. Can't be changed. So now what are you going to do?" Alicia's eyes met his. "You only have one choice. You have to keep going."

"To where?" She made moving on after Simone's

death sound so simple when in fact it was the most painful thing he'd ever done. "To what?"

"Now that's the hard part," she said very quietly.

By the sound of her voice, Jack had a hunch Alicia had gone through a dark time of her own.

"When you're brought to your knees, what do you grab on to? What do you use as your reason for going on, for not giving up? You have to have something to cling to or you'll sink into a black pit of bitterness and depression." Her gaze slid from him to the rippling water beyond.

Jack realized then that Alicia understood where he was in his life. He saw it in the rigid line of her shoulders, in the way her restless fingers threaded and undid. From the faraway look on her face, he knew she'd slid back to a bad time in her life and saw again the struggles she'd surmounted. Once more Jack yearned to know more about her. Alicia might have sank into the black pit she spoke of, just as he had. But somehow she'd pulled herself out.

"What happened to you?" he murmured.

For a moment she didn't move. Then slowly her head turned and she looked straight into his eyes, her own black with secrets.

Tell me, he urged silently.

"It doesn't matter what puts you there, Jack," she said in a soft voice. "What matters is that you let God pull you out and help you get on with your life."

"I'm not sure I can do that," he admitted.

A slow smile transformed her face.

"That's what I'm saying. *You* can't. God can." She rose, emptied the dregs of her coffee onto the sand and shoved her cup into her bag. "I better get back to work."

Jack walked beside her, silently mulling over their conversation as they climbed the hill. At his truck he stopped, put a hand on her arm. She drew away immediately but he ignored that.

"Thanks, Alicia."

"I didn't do anything." She smiled at him. "But you're welcome."

He let her walk about ten yards before he called her name. She paused, turned and raised one eyebrow in a question.

"Don't you think we should have a planning session about the sod house soon?"

A troubled look filled her face. She nibbled on her bottom lip for several minutes before she finally nodded. "When? Where?"

"Tomorrow night? At Lives so we can include the boys?" When she nodded again he checked with his sister, then turned back to Alicia. "I'll pick you up at seven."

"Okay. I'll be ready." She studied him a few seconds more, then, with her long-legged stride, she crossed the road and quickly jogged toward her shop.

Almost as if she was running away.

From him? He hoped not.

Jack climbed into his truck, determined to ignore the curiosity that burgeoned inside him about this amazing woman.

"Do you remember anything about my case, Mrs. Endersley?" Having poured out her history, Alicia held her breath, hoping against hope.

Please, God...

"I have a murky memory of you and later, of placing your baby—a boy, wasn't it?" the social worker finally said in a thoughtful tone.

"Yes, that's right." Excitement bubbled inside Alicia. Maybe at last—

"But I don't recall where I placed him," Mrs. Endersley said. "And I wouldn't be able to find out because I'm retired now. I have no access to the records. You'd have to go through channels."

"What does that mean?" Alicia's frustration built as the woman described a number of forms the government required to release information, forms she couldn't fill out without asking for help. Doing that would reveal her illiteracy.

"But even if you do go through all that, I'm not sure anyone would tell you where the child is now," Mrs. Endersley said.

"Why not?" Alicia felt her stomach drop. "I only want to make sure he's safe, loved."

"I'm sure you do," the social worker said in a mollifying tone. "But remember, you signed a document giving up all right to know anything more about him."

"I did?" Alicia tried to recall it, but she'd suppressed the memories from those awful days too well. "I can't remember."

"What year did you say it was?" Mrs. Endersley listened, then sighed. "Yes, you would have signed that document. They were mandatory then. We couldn't have given your baby to the adoption agency without such a form. Now, of course, things are often much more lenient. People are more willing to work out a way for the birth mother to keep in touch...." Her voice trailed away.

Alicia felt her tenuous grasp on the lead to her child slipping away. But she couldn't give up yet.

"You're saying there's no way for me to find out where my son is?" The weight of not knowing pressed down on her shoulders. "No way at all?" she pleaded.

"The only thing I can think of, other than filling out the papers I told you about and waiting to see if the government grants your request, is to personally contact the adoption agency and ask if they'll release the information to you," Mrs. Endersley said. "I must tell you that's unlikely, unless there's a pressing reason, like a life-or-death situation. Even then it doesn't happen often. Only once in my memory, in fact."

"I wouldn't know who to contact. I don't know

what agency you used," Alicia wailed as her heart dropped further.

"We used several. Let me think about it for a few days and see if I can remember which one I chose for your son."

Alicia thanked her and reluctantly hung up the phone. Before she could run to the back of her shop and grab her purse to meet Jack, it rang again. Thinking the woman had forgotten some important fact, Alicia grabbed it eagerly.

"Alicia, it's Nancy. Have you got a minute?" her friend asked. From the tone of her voice, Alicia knew she had to make time despite the fact that she was already very late and Jack would be waiting to pick her up so they could go to the meeting.

"For you? Of course I have time. How are you and Harold?" she asked, glad to hear a friendly voice.

"We're fine. No, we're worried," Nancy corrected. "Mr. Parcet came to the Friendship Center this morning. He pretended he was there about a donation, but that wasn't true."

"It wasn't?" Prickles went up on the back of Alicia's neck.

"No." Nancy's voice hardened. "He asked too many questions and he left without giving us a cent."

Alicia's blood froze. Her mouth went dry.

"He was trying to get information," Nancy said. The Friendship Center was a gathering place where those with Aboriginal heritage came to enjoy coffee with a friendly face, or perhaps to check out the local job situation, or to use the resources Nancy and Harold offered for free. Alicia had worked there before she'd come to Churchill. Mr. Parcet would have no business there, but clearly he'd uncovered her connection with Nancy and Harold.

"Did anyone tell him anything?" she whispered.

"I doubt anyone there knows enough to tell." Nancy's calm demeanor was definitely ruffled. "You've been in Churchill for seven years and you haven't kept in touch with anyone back here but us, have you?"

"No. So I don't have to worry." Alicia licked her lips as hope simmered inside.

"Not worry," Nancy agreed. "But you should be aware that he's pulling out all the stops to find you. I told you, this is important to him. He wants that money."

Silence stretched between them as each remembered that awful time so long ago. Finally Alicia found her voice.

"I've been trying to figure out where the baby was placed, to make sure he's safe. I contacted my former social worker but she doesn't remember." She exhaled her frustration. "I haven't any more leads, but there's a man here who's trying to find his daughter's birth mother. He gave me a website address. Could you do some research on your computer?"

"I'd love to, Alicia. I want to make sure your child is out of that man's reach as much as you do," Nancy said in a hard tone.

"Thanks. I don't know how useful this will be, but it can't hurt to check it out. I never imagined it would be so difficult to uncover an adoption." She turned to find Jack walking toward her. She'd been so intent on the conversation she hadn't heard him enter. How much had he heard? "I have to go, Nancy."

"I'll call you as soon as I learn something," her friend promised.

"I'll call you soon. Thanks for the warning." Alicia hung up, collecting herself as she did. But when she glanced at Jack, her smile faltered. His eyes gave away his irritation.

"When you called you said you'd be ten minutes," he said with an edge to his voice. "I've been waiting for ages." He tossed a meaningful glance at her clock.

"I know and I apologize." Alicia sought for conciliatory words. "I was already running late and then I had back-to-back phone calls, important calls. I couldn't ignore them. I'm so sorry, Jack. I know your time is valuable and I appreciate you offering to work with me on the sod house project." Relief flooded her that he wasn't asking questions about whatever he'd overheard. "I'm ready now." She grabbed her jacket and her handbag.

Alicia hadn't eaten supper, but hopefully Laurel would have the usual evening snack for the boys and she could eat that. If not, she'd make some toast later.

"Ignore my bad mood, okay? Everybody gets caught on a call sometimes, especially if you're self-employed." Jack sighed heavily, rolled his shoulders and stretched his neck from one side to the other. "You're the chairman. The meeting can hardly start without you."

Alicia wanted to ask what had prompted his bad mood but figured now was not the time. She also ignored the opportunity to explain her phone call. Instead she followed him outside, locked the store door and climbed into his tired old truck.

When they were finally moving toward Lives, she asked, "Do you want to tell me what's wrong?"

"No." He grimaced. "It's been a lousy day. I don't know if I'm going to be much use tonight."

She leaned back. "Such a gorgeous evening. I should have walked to Lives and saved you the trouble of waiting for me."

"That's a long walk," he said, studying her for a moment. "Have you done it before?"

"Sure. I like to walk. There's freedom in getting outside and heading in any direction you want." She saw a question in the glance he shot her way and wished she'd kept silent.

"Maybe *I* should have walked." He clamped his lips together as if to stem the rest of his remarks.

"You know, Jack, sometimes talking helps," she offered.

"Talking about Simone never seems to help," he said, his voice hard.

"Because you're angry at God." Ah, so it was about his wife. Alicia tried to think of something helpful.

"It's not just anger," Jack said as he turned onto the road leading to Lives. "It's also frustration, maybe even disappointment. I trusted God for many years. But now it feels like He let me down. What was the point of her death?" Jack shook his head. "I don't even know what to say to comfort Giselle when she starts crying."

"Why do you have to say anything?" Alicia murmured.

"Because that's my job. I'm her father," Jack said in a tight voice. "I'm supposed to make it better."

"Do you honestly think you can do that?" she said quietly. "What can you possibly say or do that would make losing her mother acceptable?"

Jack was silent for several minutes. Finally he gave her a lopsided smile. "How did you get so smart?"

"I'm not smart. Just experienced. After I lost my parents, I had a hard time. I was raised to depend on my faith, yet, for the first time in my life I couldn't make it work. I didn't *feel* like a Christian.

I felt abandoned, angry at God—probably a lot like you've been feeling," she admitted. "And I got stuck, mired in those feelings."

"So? What changed?" He pulled in next to Laurel's van at Lives Under Construction and switched off the key. Then he turned to face her, waiting.

"A friend helped me understand that even if I knew why my parents had died, they'd still be gone and I'd still be alone." Alicia smiled. "She said I needed a controlled burn so I could get on with my life."

Jack blinked. His eyes widened. "A—"

"Controlled burn," she repeated with a grin. "You've heard reports about all the recent forest fires, haven't you? How they rage uncontrollably?" She waited for his nod. "Well, this friend of mine is a fire management specialist in the Yukon. She believes in being proactive, burning some of the forest before a wildfire uses it as tinder and goes out of control. She suggested I practice being similarly proactive in my personal life."

"Uh, I don't see—" Jack's confusion was evident in his blue eyes. She could get lost staring into those gorgeous blue eyes.

Focus, Alicia.

"Basically she meant I should face the loss, get angry if I needed to and rant till I had nothing left. She advised me to get rid of all the pent up garbage that was festering inside me, then do whatever it took to get to the next stage of living." She shrugged. "So I did and was finally able to move on with my life."

Alicia wouldn't tell him she'd had to go through the same process after Mr. Parcet's attack or that those wounds had never fully healed. Jack didn't need to know about her pathetic past and, besides, she didn't want to see him withdraw with horror on his face the way people who knew about her past always did.

"She sounds like a good friend." He pulled his keys from the ignition. "Is that who you were talking to about finding the adopted person you're looking for?"

He said it so matter-of-factly it took Alicia a moment to realize he had heard part of her telephone conversation. Hopefully he hadn't heard her ask Nancy to look up that website. She couldn't imagine admitting to Jack that she was unable to read.

"Don't tell me if you don't want, Alicia. I'm not trying to pry."

"I was talking to my friend Nancy. She's not the fire management specialist. She works with Native people." Alicia wasn't going to say any more. "Shall we go in? I hate to waste Laurel's time. She's so busy, but we must include her in this."

"Yes." Jack walked with her toward the door. "If it concerns Laurel's boys, it concerns her." He knocked once, then held the door open for her.

Alicia walked through, mentally steeling herself for the rush of feeling being near him always brought. She also tried to mentally prepare for the meeting ahead. She didn't know Jack well, but she knew him enough to recognize that he was organized, liked lists and would question anything his detective brain found puzzling.

She'd have to be on guard lest she give herself away.

Alicia ignored the voice in her head that demanded to know why it was so important she didn't give handsome Jack Campbell reason to think less of her. Just because she felt this buzz inside whenever he was around didn't mean he could ever be more than a friend. Besides, she wasn't comfortable around men. Hadn't been since the attack.

Yet somehow Jack was different. Was that why she'd begun to accept courtesies from him that she'd always spurned? Her skin prickled when Jack's fingers curled around her elbow, but not because she was afraid of him. More because she had this inner certainty that Jack wouldn't hurt her. Was the buzz he caused due to the attraction that continued to grow despite her efforts to quell it?

Jack was always nice to her. But he was just being polite, nothing more. She knew that.

Still, it couldn't hurt to be polite back, could it?

He would be just another friend. So why did she yearn for more than friendship from this man?

Chapter Seven

As far as information gathering went, Jack found the evening's discussion enlightening. Once launched on the topic of the sod house, Alicia recited stories with details she'd never before mentioned. Jack scribbled wildly. But when she finally paused, he realized he still didn't have what he wanted.

"So can we say we'll build a fifteen-by-twenty-foot floor area?" he asked with a flicker of frustration.

"Is it important we decide size right now?" Alicia asked quietly.

"I think so." He reined in his irritation. "If we're going to get this done in time, we should start firming up the details."

"Oh." Alicia nibbled on her bottom lip, looking adorably confused.

"It doesn't have to be an exact replica, does it, Jack?" Laurel interjected. She'd always been good at mediating solutions. "I mean, this is supposed to be a representation, something to give an idea of how it *might* have looked."

"Yes." Alicia smiled at both of them. "The thing is, Jack, the size will be determined by how deeply we can dig, when we hit permafrost and what kind of soil we're into. It will also depend on the driftwood we can scavenge. We may have to approach local businesses for donations."

"I see." Jack scribbled more notes, added question marks beside some, then noticed Alicia hadn't brought a notebook. "Would you like some paper?" He prepared to tear a few sheets off his own pad.

"No," she looked away from him. "We don't need more than one secretary, do we?"

Hoping she wouldn't want to rehash everything again next time because she hadn't made any notes, Jack shrugged.

"I guess I could type my notes and email everyone a copy," he said.

"I don't have email," Alicia said.

"Really?" Shocked, Jack caught himself staring at her. Her chin thrust out as if she was preparing to weather a put-down. Funny how he hated seeing that defensiveness.

"I can't afford a computer yet," she murmured. "Eli's been managing my website from here."

"That's nice of him." Jack nodded at the boy.

"Then I'll drop off a copy of my notes at Tansi. Or Giselle can."

"Okay." Alicia sounded strange.

"I don't understand where the driftwood comes into it," Laurel murmured.

"Most of what you described sounds entirely different from what we did in Vancouver," Jack added. "Maybe you can explain it so we understand better."

"Sure." Alicia nodded. "But it's not very complicated."

"It's not?" Jack frowned. The house he and Simone had helped with had seemed quite complicated, especially when it came to cutting the sod.

"No." Alicia grinned at him. "You see, the name 'sod' house isn't exactly accurate. The first settlers didn't find much sod around here. But they needed a quick project to give them shelter so they copied the prairie sod house model because it's fast. They started by digging shallow holes in the ground."

"Tools?" he asked, scribbling as fast as he could.

"Very few," Alicia said. "A pick to dig. A wedge to split logs. An adze to shape the planks they made and a snow knife to cut blocks of snow for the porch. Maybe you should give me a piece of paper. I'll try to sketch it."

Jack tore out a sheet and handed it to her. In ten seconds she'd outlined out a structure.

"They dug a shallow trench then split driftwood to make a frame. Planks on the floor raised it to give warmth off the frozen ground." She bent intently over her sketch, her hair falling to one side as she worked, her fingers swift and sure.

Jack couldn't stop staring at her; she looked so lovely. Until he noticed Laurel was watching him. Then he pulled his gaze back to Alicia's drawing.

"As I understand it," she said, her focus completely on her sketch, "they laid the planks vertically to make short walls and then a roof. They mixed whatever bits of sod they could find, probably moss with dirt as well, and piled it on the walls and roof. Once the snow fell, they cut blocks and laid them over the entrance tunnel creating a long porch that helped keep the wind from blowing straight into the house."

With a flourish she finished her sketch and held it up.

"It's completely different than I expected." Jack admired the way she'd created perspective so he could see exactly how the thing was formed. "It almost resembles an igloo."

"It probably did look like that in the winter," she murmured, her head tilted to one side. "Snow would have added insulation." The easy way she added the details told Jack that Alicia didn't need the books he'd been so intent on.

"You seem to know all the details." He was ashamed he'd doubted her.

"I made the elder repeat the process," Alicia

admitted, her cheeks flushed, her eyes avoiding his. "I wanted to be certain I understood exactly how this came together, to be as accurate as possible."

"You did a good job." He could tell she was embarrassed by his compliment so he changed the subject. "Our first step, then, would be to collect some driftwood."

"Yes." She did lift her lashes then and flashed her beautiful smile at him. "I've already pulled some from the water." She said it as if it had been the easiest task in the world for her to haul waterlogged trees from the frigid bay. "I found some big ones that David Tutu pulled to shore with his boat. But we'll need more."

Jack's admiration for Alicia grew. Far from being unprepared, Alicia was organized and far ahead of the points on his list.

"I hope you won't mind, but I also asked a chief I know to make an adze for us. I met his mom in Thompson a couple of months ago. She also gave me a lot of information."

Jack winced. He'd mentally criticized Alicia for disorganization, but she'd made the long and tiring journey all the way to Thompson to get firsthand information so she'd be able to be accurate in her recreation. Jack figured he was going to have to up his game to keep pace with this plucky woman. Anticipation coursed through him. This might be fun.

"So when and where do we start?" he asked.

"I haven't been successful with that." She chewed her bottom lip. The way she cast her eyes lower told him someone had put down her idea to recreate the sod house. "Town council keeps putting me off. Last time they suggested I use a piece of land that's a long way out of town."

"You don't want that?" Jack watched her, waiting for her complaint against the council. It didn't come.

"It's a good spot." The smooth skin between her eyebrows pleated. "It could work. But it's so far from what's going on in town. My goal is to tie the opening of the sod house to a town event. That should build tourist interest and maybe bring them back to view future projects that I know the boys will create."

"It would also be a talking point around town as the kids construct it," Jack said, catching Alicia's vision. He turned to his sister. "Do you have any sway with the mayor or council?"

"Not really." Laurel made a face. "Some of them still worry the boys might attack the town while it sleeps." She grinned when the boys hooted with laughter. "They'd probably like it to be built out here."

Alicia shook her head. "Sod houses are part of the *town's* history," she emphasized.

"Then I guess it's up to me," Jack said. "I'm a newcomer so I don't know how much help I'll be," he warned. "But maybe I can persuade them to include a paragraph about it in promotional packages for the town."

Funny how the sudden brightening of Alicia's face made *him* happier. As if making Alicia Featherstone's dreams come true was his job.

That told Jack he was getting too involved. And yet, he couldn't deny Alicia's project intrigued him. He liked that it would involve the Lives boys in a very positive way. Even better, he'd be part of teaching cooperation and how to make something worthwhile.

But was the real reason Jack was anxious to get started on the sod house because he was looking forward to getting to know Alicia Featherstone more personally? While the others enjoyed Laurel's buffet of snacks, Jack searched his heart.

The day he'd buried Simone lay too sharp in his memory, the awful gutting of his heart too painful to repeat. He could never again allow any woman to become that special, because he knew he could never again survive the grief. He'd only survived this time because Giselle needed him.

And yet—

At the end of their meeting, long after he'd dropped Alicia at her door, hours after he'd finished a steaming latte on his deck, Jack couldn't quite dismiss the memory of her dark eyes brimming with excitement.

Nor could he forget the pathos he'd heard in her voice when she'd been talking on the phone earlier.

I never imagined it would be so difficult to uncover an adoption.

Alicia had said she was searching for someone. Jack suddenly wondered if Alicia might be looking for her own birth parent. Nothing else made sense.

In that moment his heart melted. Alicia was an older version of Giselle—desperate to know the people who'd given her life.

And Jack wanted to help her. He wanted it badly.

He wanted it so much he almost didn't hear the voice in the back of his mind warning him that from now on, he'd have to keep it strictly business between himself and Alicia, create some distance between them.

For his own self-preservation.

"You *are* going to tell me the whereabouts of your half-breed kid."

Two weeks later, Alicia almost dropped the phone as fear crawled up her spine. Then a part of her sleep-deprived brain repeated Nancy's long ago calming voice.

You're not a victim, Alicia. You're a survivor. You know the truth now. God is greater than any man. He is your defender. 'Greater is He that is in you.'

"You might as well tell me, Alicia." The sharp

edge in Mr. Parcet's voice was like a rasp over her nerves. "We both know I always get what I want."

"Not this time." Unable to stomach his snide voice a second longer, she did the only thing she could. She hung up.

She got out of bed but couldn't shake the chill that followed her as she dressed. When the phone rang again a moment later, Alicia ignored it, frozen by a thousand churning emotions, all of them iced with fear. Where could she go to get away from him? How could she stop him?

God?

There was a click as the answering machine switched on. Her whole body went rigid in antici-pation of his sneering words.

"Alicia? It's Jack." After a pause he exhaled heav-ily. "Okay, I guess you're out. I wanted to drop off the notes from our meeting the other night, but since you're not there I'll stick them in the door. Don't forget we're meeting at the coffee shop at four to strategize our meeting with town council tonight." A pause, then he hung up.

Jack. Alicia's heartbeat kept on racing, but for a different reason. The meeting at Laurel's had been two nights ago and she still couldn't suppress the tiny tremor that thinking of him always brought. She let the air whoosh out of her lungs and leaned weakly against the cool plaster wall, trying to even out her breathing.

As she focused on Jack, the dirty, damaged feelings revived by Mr. Parcet slowly slid away. She inhaled a cleansing breath from the pot of sage nearby, poured a fresh cup of coffee and carried it outside to her tiny upstairs balcony. There she snuggled in the tired old lawn chair she'd rescued and rebuilt, and savored the rich brew. She gazed over Hudson Bay, silently begging God to send His comforting peace and a way to break free of Mr. Parcet.

The train whistle signaled its arrival at the station. Alicia should be downstairs with her shop door open, ready for the morning's business. She couldn't afford to sit here, wasting time, trying to pretend her world hadn't just fallen apart at its carefully sewn seams.

But she couldn't pretend normal right now. Not after that call, not when *he'd* found her. She felt scared and more uncertain about her security in God than she ever had.

"Where are You? Why don't You help me?" she whispered, studying the fleeting puffs of cloud as if they held the answers she craved. "How do I deal with him? How do I protect my child? Where *is* my child?"

No answer. Just that same verse kept running through her head.

Be still and know that I am God. What did it mean?

It was so hard to learn about God when she

couldn't read the Bible for herself. She closed her eyes and remembered that Pastor Rick had used that reference on Sunday. He'd said Jesus was sleeping in the boat and the storm roused him. He'd been angry and Rick had said He'd ordered the storm to stop. Rick had said that translated, the words "be still," which Jesus used, carried a connotation similar to "shut up."

"Meaning I'm supposed to shut up and let God handle it?" Alicia let the idea percolate through her brain. What was the verse Rick had used? Psalms 37:7.

"Be still before the Lord and wait patiently for him; fret not yourself over the one who prospers in his way, over the man who carries out evil devices!" Meaning Mr. Parcet?

Nancy would say God was telling her He had everything under control so she should stop fretting. Easy to say. Hard to do.

Then her mother's favorite verse from Psalms 131 floated through Alicia's head.

"But I have calmed and quieted my soul, like a weaned child with its mother; like a weaned child is my soul within me."

God knew all about Mr. Parcet. He knew her son's whereabouts and He would look after her in His own time.

Alicia repeated the verses over and over, desperate to find peace. But though she tried to let it all go, tried to "shut up" and give it to God, her soul remained troubled. She had to learn to read because memorized verses were no longer enough. She needed to be able to search the scriptures for herself.

Unsettled, Alicia rose. Time to go to work. As she turned to go inside, she heard someone call her name. Jack stood below, watching her.

"So that's why you don't answer your phone." He sounded depressed.

"Guess I missed it," she said, secretly delighted to see him but puzzled by his attitude. "Where are you off to?"

He muttered something she couldn't understand.

"Sorry. I can't hear you. Wait a second. I'll come down." She left her dirty cup on the kitchen counter then rushed down the inside stairs and out the back door. An inner voice warned, *Too eager,* which didn't temper her impatience one bit. "What did you say?"

Jack's face was now a darker tan than when he'd arrived. In Alicia's opinion it only added to his handsome good looks. Then she noticed his perspiration-dotted forehead.

"Oh, you're out running," she guessed. "I'm sorry if I stopped you." The apology had barely left her mouth when she noticed what he was carrying. "Isn't that the kite Giselle bought yesterday?"

"Yes." He held it as if it was hot.

"Is something wrong with it?" she asked. "I'll replace it if there is."

"It's fine," he mumbled. Clearly he did not want to explain.

Since she hadn't seen Jack in days she'd decided he was avoiding her. Which was understandable. She figured she wasn't the kind of woman he was used to.

But that didn't help her figure out how to control the crazy feelings that made her feel dazed whenever he was near. And she could hardly ask somebody for advice.

"I'm glad we're meeting to strategize," she told him. "I'm a little worried about meeting with the town council."

"Why should you worry?" His tone offered quiet understanding. "They're just ordinary men."

"But I'm not educated like them. I never even finished school." As soon as the words left her tongue she knew she shouldn't have said them. She so didn't want Jack to think less of her, and yet she knew he would if he knew she'd been raped and given away her baby.

"That must have been very hard for you." He seemed genuinely sympathetic, which she appreciated. But he didn't know the worst about her.

"I manage. Anyway, thanks for leaving the notes." Not that she could read them.

Jack studied her as if he couldn't think what to

say. He shuffled his feet, which were clad in sturdy hikers. Alicia seized on the much-needed change in topic.

"New boots, huh?" she said, tongue in cheek.

"Yes, you were right. My old ones are no good around town, so I'm saving them for when I'm inside the hotel." Jack didn't give her the snappy comeback she expected. In fact, a muscle in his jaw flickered. "I have to go now."

"Okay." Alicia stood in place, mystified.

"Aren't you going to ask where I'm going?" Jack asked.

"Um—" Puzzled by his tone, she shook her head.

"I'll tell you anyway. I have to go figure out how to fly this stupid kite you sold my daughter." He certainly wasn't joking. His blue eyes were cool. "Because *you* entered us in the father/daughter kite flying event on Canada Day."

"Because Giselle asked me to." Alicia caught a flicker in his eyes. Truth dawned. "You don't know how to fly a kite."

"No, I don't." Jack looked embarrassed.

"It's really not that hard." How Alicia longed to chuck her responsibilities, go to the cliffs with him and show him how to fly the kite. Mostly she just wanted to ease his worry. But she had to work and, anyway, at the moment he didn't look as if he'd appreciate her help. Encouragement was the best she could offer. "You can do it, Jack."

"Really?" He huffed a sigh. "It's probably a breeze for you, but I spent last night trying to get this thing in the air while Giselle was at basketball practice. I almost wrecked it."

She stepped back, surprised. Jack grimaced.

"I know it's not your fault, Alicia. It's more that I'm finally coming to terms with how incompetent I am at being a father without Simone."

"You? Incompetent as a father?" She made a sound of disgust. "Give me a break. Anyway, flying a kite isn't important when it comes to fatherhood."

"It's important to me."

"Why?" Alicia asked, confused. He had everything else. Why would a kite matter?

"Because it matters to Giselle." His voice was flat. Tiny stress lines fanned out from his eyes. "My daughter is counting on me and I'll look like an idiot because I can't get this thing airborne." He thrust the kite away from him as if it were a weapon.

"Like *you* could ever look like an idiot." She sniffed in disbelief. "You're the kind of put-together person we all admire. People like you have their lives totally on track. A kite can't ruin that."

"On track?" He barked a laugh. "Totally untrue." From the way his lips pinched together, she knew he needed more from her.

"Jack," she began gently. "The point is to have fun with your daughter. Giselle wants to spend time with *you,* not the kite. She won't care if the two of you lose."

"I'll care," he snapped.

Alicia was bewildered that this capable man doubted himself on such a little thing. She'd always envied him for his confidence.

"Why would you care?" she asked at last, sensing a world of hurt lay hidden deep inside him.

"Because I'm supposed to be in charge." Jack's eyes blazed silver-blue with anger that she guessed he'd kept buried inside ever since his wife died. "I failed to protect my wife. According to Teddy, I'm not great at being an hotelier, either."

"I'm sure Teddy never said that," Alicia protested.

"He didn't have to. It's enough he has to tell me something ten times." He sighed. "I'm lousy at the sports people do here—hockey, football, snowshoeing—so I don't fit in. Now I can't even handle a stupid kite."

Alicia would have laughed except for what Jack said next.

"I'm the one who's supposed to make Giselle's world good and right and I'm messing that up, too."

"You mean you're supposed to make sure Giselle never loses anything again?" Alicia asked, latching on to his last sentence for the kernel of truth she heard there.

Jack's eyebrows drew together in a frown, but he nodded. "Yeah."

"You will fail at that, Jack," she said flatly. "You can't do it because it's impossible." His eyes flared but Alicia pressed on. "And the reason it's impossible is because that's not your job. You're not God. You can't control everything Giselle faces. You're not even supposed to try."

"But I am supposed to protect her," he argued.

"Not by trying to be an expert at everything she wants to try. Not by putting a fence around her and not by acting like some kind of bodyguard, taking all the hits so she won't have to." Alicia knew she'd struck a sore spot from his angry expression. "You can't do it, Jack. But even if you could protect her from everything, should you?"

"What do you mean?" Jack demanded.

"Giselle is growing up. Part of growing up is figuring out how to handle problems." She smiled at him. "I'm pretty sure your dad wasn't there to run interference every time you ran into a problem, was he?"

"No, but it's different with Giselle." Jack's shoulders sagged from the burden he carried. "She doesn't have her mom anymore and this silly search for her birth mother has left her very insecure."

"It hasn't left her insecure in her certainty that you are there for her." Alicia held his gaze. "And it isn't a silly search. It's part of figuring out her identity. Giselle knows you're in her corner if she needs you. She has no doubt about your love."

"Maybe not," he agreed. "But love isn't everything. The rest of it—"

"Love is the part that counts," she told him in a stern voice. "The rest of it she'll handle as the issues come up. That's how you raised her." She smiled at him.

"You think?" he asked dubiously.

Alicia nodded her head.

"I know. Your daughter will do fine, as long as you're there when she needs you, Jack. Winning a kite-flying contest won't affect her ability to overcome things one little bit. It certainly isn't going to affect the way she looks at you." She tilted her head to one side, studying him. "But I think you already know that. You just needed someone to remind you it's true."

Jack stared at her for a long time, silent, his blue eyes searching hers. Alicia knew she had to go. She had a business to run. But how could she leave him like this—confused, needy?

Jack needy? Mocking laughter filled her head.

"You're right, Alicia. I'm overreacting." He squeezed his eyes closed, tilted his head back and rolled his shoulders. "You must think I'm nuts."

"I think you're a nice guy who wants the best for his daughter. What's wrong with that?" She could hear voices getting closer. "I'm sorry but I've got to go open my shop. See you at four?"

"Yeah."

Alicia could feel his eyes burning into her back until she finally closed the back door behind her. Someone was rapping on the glass. Pushing away all thoughts of handsome Jack Campbell, she hurried to open her business.

Wasn't it silly that she could hardly wait until she'd see him again at four o'clock? As if she needed Jack in her world to make things better.

Chapter Eight

Jack could hardly tamp down his anticipation. It was ten past four. What was taking Alicia so long?

A little bubble of happiness floated up from inside when she finally pushed through the café door, her dark hair streaming behind her. Funny to be so glad she'd left it loose.

"The wind's picked up," she said in a breathless tone as she sat down across from him. "It's a good thing I'm strong. Otherwise, it would have blown me down the street."

Her cheeks flushed and she slid her thick lashes down to hide her gaze from him. He thought she looked beautiful.

"Alicia, you are the most solid, firmly planted woman I've ever known." Jack smiled, for once allowing his admiration to show. "I don't think there's anything that could faze you."

"Uh—" She was obviously discomfited by his compliment.

He scanned her shapely figure, shown to perfection in her red dress.

"You look fantastic."

"You don't have to say that, but thank you." She brushed it off as if she didn't believe him, and for a moment that bugged him.

Jack couldn't figure it out until he thought over their past conversations and recalled several times in which she'd made fleeting but denigrating comments about herself. Alicia always seemed so self-assured and confident, he'd assumed she was joking.

Yet, at this moment, nothing in her eyes or her expression looked the least amused. Perhaps no one had ever complimented her. Jack scoffed at himself and tossed aside that thought. With her dark beauty, he'd seen the admiring glances Alicia drew wherever she went.

"Take it from me that you are a very beautiful woman." When she blushed again and her lashes fluttered down, Jack decided that in the future he'd pay more attention to what went on behind her dark, impenetrable stare.

"Thanks." Her eyes veered away from his. "This coffee is excellent. I haven't tasted the caramel flavor before."

"It's my favorite." Jack admired the way her brown eyes glowed when she smiled. Her lashes lowered as she savored a second swallow. "So about the meeting tonight," he began, struggling to find a way to explain what he'd done.

"I'm really nervous," Alicia admitted. "I told you I wanted the land beside the old stone house, didn't I?"

"Several times." He leaned back, waiting. "Why?"

"Someone started building that place forty years ago. It looks so desolate, perched on the beachhead like that, still unfinished," she explained. "It's an excellent tourist draw. If we built our sod house beside it, I think we'd get a lot of traffic."

Our sod house. Jack liked the sound of that.

"The thing is," Alicia murmured, her brows drawn together, "Will Sweetwater is a prominent voice on council and he's against using that land, even though it would be perfect."

"What makes that tract so desirable?" Jack wondered aloud.

"Several things. It's easier to dig there than most other viable places. I checked it out." She winked at him. His heart gave a bump of pleasure, glad to share in the excitement shining on her face. "Though you'd better not tell anyone that. I've been planning this project for a long time, Jack. I wanted my facts straight before I talked to council. But facts don't help much with Will—"

"Alicia," he said, holding up a hand to cut in. "I, um, did something."

"Oh." Her eyes narrowed—with fear? "Is it something…bad?"

That slight hesitation told Jack she was afraid, though she worked hard not to show it, to pretend she was tough enough to take it. In spite of her efforts, her innocence, her transparency shone through. Such an attractive quality.

"Did you hear they've nixed the project or something?"

"No, nothing like that." His breath snagged in his throat. How would she react? "Our meeting with council tonight has been canceled."

"Canceled?" Her shoulders sagged. "They don't think I can do it, do they?" Defeat colored her voice. He realized he hated that sound.

"Oh, they know you can do it, Alicia." When a tiny smile flickered at the corner of her mouth, Jack felt a rush of pride that he'd been privileged to meet this incredible woman.

He wasn't sure his meeting with some town council members this afternoon had been impromptu. Laurel had invited him for coffee and then had to leave, but not before she'd introduced him to some men, two of them town council members, who were discussing Alicia's request for the land. Jack had grabbed the opportunity to emphasize the soundness of it in economic terms the men would appreciate—tourism.

"Alicia, they've agreed to give you the land you want, next to that abandoned stone house," he said.

"Really?" Her eyes grew wide. "Are you sure?"

At his nod, she tipped her head back and laughed, her delight obvious. "Amazing."

Jack wasn't sure how much he should say and how long her questions would take. Apparently not long at all, he realized, as he noticed a tiny frown pleat her forehead.

"How do you know this, Jack?" Suspicion threaded her question.

He forced his face to remain impassive. It was imperative he phrase this just right or she would think he'd interfered in a project she'd poured her heart into perfecting. He didn't want that.

Of course, he wanted to get on with building the sod house, but behind Jack's real motivation, behind his focused sales pitch to the council members was a need to somehow repay the kindness Alicia had shown to Giselle. Because of her, his daughter had taken a strong interest in her new home and the history surrounding it. Because of her, Giselle was happy. Because of Alicia his world was so much better.

"Jack?" Alicia prompted. "What's wrong?"

"Nothing. I overheard some men at the coffee shop talking about the sod house plan we're supposed to present tonight. So I butted in and gave my opinion." Choosing his words with care and keeping his own role minimized, Jack explained what had happened in broad terms. "Once they visited the site with me and I could show them what you plan and how it will impact tourism here, they were definitely in favor."

"I see." She stared into her cup.

Jack fretted that Alicia was offended by his interference until her eyes met his. A tremulous smile lifted her full lips. His heart rate ramped up.

"I know you're not telling me everything," she said quietly, holding his gaze. "I know you did a lot of convincing. Thank you."

Her insight surprised Jack, but he shrugged it off. "I didn't do much."

"So does this mean we can finally get started?" The question held undertones, as if she was afraid to trust that her dream was about to come true.

"They said they'd formalize things tonight and that the permit would be ready tomorrow," Jack told her, smugly satisfied by her now-blazing grin. "Let the sod house begin."

"Oh, Jack." Impulsively she leaned forward, grabbed his hand and squeezed it, her face radiant with joy. "The boys are so excited about actually building something with their own hands and showing people they're not useless and damaged as some say they are. They're going to be over the moon."

"I'm glad I could help."

"So am I," she murmured.

His fingers automatically curled around hers as a spark of warmth shot up his arm straight to his heart. Jump-started, it began pounding like a jackhammer. A hard tiny place deep inside Jack softened and melted as Alicia's beauty magnified, enhanced by the tremulous smile that lifted her lips. Her gaze held his with an invisible thread from which he couldn't break free. And didn't want to.

"I can't believe God has finally answered my prayer," she whispered. A tiny tear glistened at the corner of her eye before tumbling onto their clasped hands. "He used you to do it, Jack."

Her face bloomed with color as she glanced at their joined hands. She eased hers away. At least she didn't jerk away as she had before. He was glad of that. But then her words penetrated his brain.

God? Had used *him?* Jack almost laughed. Unwilling to shatter her bubble of happiness, he let her words go without challenge. Let her revel in this first step to accomplishing her goal. He'd bask in her joy.

"Since we don't have to attend a council meeting, I think we should hold a meeting with the boys tonight." Jack smiled at Alicia's eager nod. "I'll call Laurel and ask if it's okay." He made the call, delighted when Laurel enthusiastically approved. "It's on, Alicia."

"Great. Maybe we can begin digging this weekend. The boys don't have many days of school left," she said. "They'll soon be free to start excavating." She frowned. "But will you be able to get away from the hotel?"

"Yes. I'm finally starting to get the hang of things," Jack told her.

"That's a change. Before, you seemed so down," she reminded.

"I was." He shrugged. "Teddy read me the riot act. I still have lots to learn but I'm beginning to realize that a mistake isn't the end of the earth." He accepted a refill from the waitress who walked by. "You know when Giselle and I spent last Christmas with Laurel, I was already looking for a new career. It was Teddy who suggested I take over the hotel. He said May would be the best time to start because I'd have plenty of time to learn the ropes. He was right."

"Teddy would know. I think he looked at buying the place himself at one time." Alicia leaned back in her chair, as relaxed now as he'd ever seen her.

"So that's how he knows so much about the place," Jack murmured. "I'm very grateful for Teddy. He's helping me understand that Churchill is a niche market. Many of the things I thought necessary don't apply, and some things I'd never thought of doing are what Teddy calls 'value added.' They could help with my return on investment."

"So meeting Teddy was a God-incidence?" Alicia asked, her lips twitching in a teasing smile that only added to her beauty.

"Maybe." Jack wouldn't go into that. "Teddy keeps telling me to lighten up, that most visitors expect rough conditions here. He claims that what they're really looking for when they finally arrive in Churchill isn't a five-star palace but a warm welcome, as if they're among family."

"Isn't that what we're all looking for?" Her smile dimmed.

The tone of her voice, the shadows in her dark eyes, the way she stared into the distance all made Jack wonder if Alicia, in spite of her aura of independence, was lonely. "It'll be nice to work on this project with you," he said, and marveled that it was true.

Funny how only a short time ago he hadn't really wanted to get involved with the sod house. Now he could hardly wait to start working with Alicia. Jack had a hunch that despite any issue they might run into, she would surmount it, keep her promise and make sure the sod house was complete before the mid-August deadline.

Jack hadn't known her long, but he'd gained a world of insight into Alicia Featherstone. He'd learned she had a reputation around town for seeking out the old, the infirm and the needy, and then she set about enriching their lives. Simple things like putting up bird feeders so an old man could sit at his window to watch, or organizing a community sewing group to create stuffed animals for kids who had to leave Churchill for medical treatment.

Alicia was a proud woman who put action behind

her talk. She wholeheartedly embraced the value her culture placed on people. Perseverance and determination defined Alicia Featherstone, and Jack's admiration for her grew daily. The way she welcomed Giselle at her store and even encouraged her interest only solidified his respect for her.

But he could not allow his feelings for Alicia to grow beyond admiration and respect. Though he hadn't expected it, the raw emotions from losing Simone *were* diminishing. But that didn't mean he could allow fondness for Alicia to grow. Along that way lay a world of hurt.

Jack was not prepared to risk loving and losing again. Never again.

And yet, if he was going to open himself to a relationship with any woman, Alicia would be the woman he chose.

Alicia tightened her fingers around the doorknob, ready to leave for her meeting with the sod house committee. She groaned when the phone pealed.

She'd be late again. But she answered the call all the same.

"Alicia, this is Mrs. Endersley. I've been thinking about your case a lot recently." The elderly woman's brisk tone said this call could be important.

"That's nice of you." Alicia swallowed, suppressing the butterfly of hope that fluttered inside her.

"I don't like gaps in my memory. I had to come

up with the answer. And I did. You son was placed by the Forest Grove Adoption Agency," she said triumphantly. "Out of Langley, British Columbia."

"Oh. Thank you for calling me back to let me know." A thrill tickled through her at the information even though Alicia wasn't sure how much it would help locate her child.

But Mrs. Endersley wasn't finished.

"I remember Margaret Brown was the director of Forest Grove back then." She paused a moment. "If you can find her, you have my permission to mention I sent you to her. That might help in your search."

"Thank you," Alicia said, sensing this was a break in the woman's usual protocol.

"I once gave up a baby for adoption myself, Alicia." Mrs. Endersley's voice softened, brimming with sympathy. "I know what it is to want to be sure the child is all right. I wish you the best of luck."

"I appreciate your help so much. You've gone above and beyond your duty. God bless you." Alicia hung up slowly, musing on the unusual call. God was answering her prayer, even if it wasn't as quickly or in the way she wanted.

She got lost in daydreams of the baby who'd been part of her life for such a short time and was still a part of her heart. How she longed to find him, to know he was safe.

The honk of a horn outside broke her introspection.

Grabbing her purse, she locked the door and hurried toward Jack's car waiting at the curb. Giselle grinned when she got in.

"Lazing around after supper?" the girl teased.

Supper? Alicia's stomach gave a loud growl as if to remind her that she'd forgotten all about eating.

"A phone call," she said, trying to ignore the persistent rumbles from her midsection when Giselle described the new taco salad recipe she'd created.

Jack glanced her way but said nothing. It was a relief to finally arrive at Lives.

Laurel invited everyone to gather around a table loaded with iced tea and freshly fried doughnuts. Alicia announced they'd soon be starting work, cheered immensely by the boys' whoops of joy. She gratefully accepted the refreshments Laurel offered then leaned back and listened to the boys' excited chatter as she savored every bite. She was about to reach for seconds when Jack called for order.

"I think Alicia should explain how we'll build this sod house," he said. Every head turned to stare at her. "Go ahead, Alicia."

Now the focus of all the attention, Alicia's stomach issued a different kind of protest. She didn't like being in the spotlight. But since she'd given great thought to each boy's strength and his possible role in the project, she might as well use this opportunity to explain her ideas. Hopefully, Jack wouldn't disagree.

"First of all, I want to make it clear that the sod house is a group effort. We're doing this together," she emphasized.

"Hear hear." Jack smiled and the world righted itself. "Together." His support built her confidence.

"Each of you has specific strengths in areas that we will need," she continued. "I want to capitalize on that, but if you don't like my idea or would prefer to do something else, please say so. Nothing's etched in stone. Okay?"

Around the table, one by one, each boy nodded.

"Good. So here's what I propose. I'll start with Garret," she said, identifying the boy to her left. "You have a way with cameras."

He lowered his eyes, embarrassed at being singled out but clearly pleased she'd noticed his skill.

"I'm hoping you will help us with construction," she reassured him, knowing how enthusiastic he'd been about the build. "But I'd also like you to create a photo journal of the creation of our sod house."

"Great idea," Jack enthused. "I've seen your work, Garret. It's excellent. We could use your pictures in a pamphlet or a display for tourists."

Alicia's heart sang at the way she and Jack meshed on this.

"Remember, that's why we're doing this—to help visitors who come to this place understand our history." She didn't want to push the boy, but she had high hopes that someone would see his work, someone who could help him advance as a photographer.

"It's quite an opportunity," Jack agreed.

"Okay." Garret shrugged as if it didn't matter, but he couldn't hide his grin.

"Great. Now, Rod. You know plants so I'd like you to research various plants in the area that might have been used for food. Matt, you're going to organize our tools. Eli, you'll help plan the sign we'll put up. Adam, I'd like you to help us collect driftwood. And Bennie, I'd like you to tape stories from some of the ancestors in the nursing home." She wanted to single out specific areas in which each boy could offer something unique, something he could later point out as his special contribution to the project. But she hadn't forgotten Giselle.

She took a sip of her iced tea, then looked at the girl who had burrowed a place in her heart.

"Giselle, you keep saying you want to learn more about the north. I believe there's a way you can do that and help out with the sod house. But it will be a lot of work." Alicia paused a moment and glanced at Jack. His face gave nothing away but she hoped he heard her warning. "Maybe you won't want to devote as much time as it will take."

"I'd like to get involved," Giselle assured her. "But I don't want to horn in on this project if the boys would rather do it themselves."

Alicia hadn't expected such sensitivity. A rush of

warmth filled her. Like her dad, Giselle knew how to touch the heart.

Eli cleared his throat.

"Like Alicia said, this is a group effort. It sounds like it's going to be a lot of work for all of us if we're to get it ready in time." He glanced sideways at Giselle, then pulled back his gaze, as if hoping no one would notice the spots of red on his cheeks. "Speaking for myself, I'm not ready to turn away any help that's offered, including yours, Giselle."

Every other boy at the table echoed his sentiment.

"Then I'd love to help however I can." Giselle shared a smile with Eli. Jack saw it and frowned. Alicia decided to keep talking.

"Thank you, Giselle. So, your focus could be on the interior and what we should put inside the sod house. You'll have to do some research to learn the kind of things the ancestors would have valued and needed, but there are library books coming and you can talk to any of the elders. Does that appeal to you?"

Giselle's dark head nodded vigorously.

"Excellent." Alicia grinned. "Now to the plan. On the last day of school, in the morning, after you guys get your report cards, I'd like you to meet me at the site."

"Which is where?" Laurel asked.

"Next to the old stone house, thanks to Jack." Alicia explained how he'd persuaded council to grant their request. His mood had dissipated. His smile brought a rush of warmth to her insides. She looked away lest he notice his effect on her. "We'll begin by marking out the dimensions. If that fits in with your plans," she said to Laurel, chagrined she hadn't considered her earlier.

"It fits perfectly." Laurel grinned. "I'll bring some packed lunches so you don't have to stop work to come back here. I know Teddy will take over for Jack. He seems totally thrilled to be so involved in the hotel. But what about you, Alicia? Who will mind your store?"

"Lucy's helping out," Alicia told her.

"Doesn't she always?" Laurel shared a smile with her. They'd both benefited from Lucy's hands-on assistance. Lucy was a part of everything in Churchill.

Alicia leaned back, savoring the boys' enthusiasm. After a moment she felt someone's eyes on her. She turned slightly to find Jack watching her. He gave her a thumbs-up, then pushed the plate of doughnuts toward her, as if he somehow knew she was still hungry. Seconds later he scooted his chair closer.

"Are you sure you're ready for this?" His breath felt warm, intimate against her ear.

Alicia drew back slightly as her gaze met his.

"With God's help, yes," she said firmly.

"I'm not sure how much help He'll be, but the kids seem gung ho." After a last quizzical look, Jack rose and walked over to Laurel. He murmured something that made her chuckle.

Some of the joy leeched out of the meeting for Alicia. The sod house was important to her, but rebuilding Jack's faith was paramount. But what could she do?

She wasn't anything to Jack, other than a co-worker on a project and a friend. Hoping otherwise was a silly schoolgirl's dream, and she'd long since given up those. Men like Jack didn't get involved with people like her.

In that moment Alicia made a decision. She'd savor the hours to come, enjoy precious moments spent working with this man who tugged at her heart and almost, almost, made her believe in happily ever after. But she wouldn't forget reality.

The reality was that she had to renew her efforts to find her son. Romance wasn't going to be part of her future.

"Excuse me, Jack. I need to take this." Two days later Alicia offered him an apologetic smile and hurried to the back of the store, the phone clutched to her ear.

To give her privacy, Jack moved to the doorway, but he didn't get far enough away. Her words floated to him, quietly intense.

"But I must find out where he is." A note of urgency made her sound passionate. "I've got to make sure he's safe, loved."

He should probably leave and come back later. But those words held him transfixed. He knew she was talking about the adopted person she'd said she was searching for, but her words told him she couldn't be looking for a birth parent. Alicia had to be searching for a child, someone she felt she needed to protect. *Her* child?

"It's not that I'm intending to *do* anything," she responded in a harried tone. "I'm sticking by the agreement I made. I just want to know he's okay."

Agreement? An adoption agreement? Jack had no time to consider that as Lucy Clow scurried past him.

"Excuse me, Jack," she puffed in a breathless greeting. "I'm late. It's so annoying to be late when Alicia is counting on me."

"You don't have to rush," he told her. "We're not on a timetable."

"Alicia's always has a timetable." Lucy smiled, her eyes twinkling. "That girl is driven to accomplish things that benefit all of us." The wind toyed with her white hair. "That's why we love her." She patted the strands back into place as she hurried away.

"You're sure there's nothing more you can tell me?" The frustration in Alicia's voice mixed with disappointment and a hint of resignation. "Send me whatever papers you think necessary then," she said finally. "If you learn anything more, this is my number."

At the sound of the phone being returned to its hook, Jack moved toward the counter where Alicia stood staring into the distance.

"Good morning." He could not tear his gaze from her proud beauty.

Alicia smiled and a burst of warmth spread through him. "Hi, Jack. Ready to make a start on our project?"

"Yes. I brought you something to energize you." He held out the large coffee cup he'd picked up at Common Grounds. "Caramel."

"My favorite. Thank you. I didn't have time to make coffee this morning so I'll really enjoy this." She took a drink and savored it until the tap of Lucy's shoes sounded her return from the back room where she'd stored her purse. "Thank you so much for helping out, Lucy."

"My pleasure. I love this place." Lucy smoothed a tender hand over a clay mask that hung behind the counter. Then she straightened. "Off you go now. Hector's already there, waiting for your instructions."

"You and your husband are godsends." Alicia hugged the small woman and pressed a kiss against her hair. "I have my cell phone if you need me."

"I won't. Go have some fun," Lucy insisted.

Jack picked up the box Alicia had left under the

front window and loaded it. Then he held open the door of his old pickup truck until she'd climbed inside. He got behind the wheel but, after a sideways look at her, decided not to interrupt whatever she was contemplating so deeply. He couldn't think of anything that wasn't a question about that phone call, so he started the truck and drove toward the stone house on the edge of town.

The boys were already there, exploring the area. To Jack's surprise, Giselle was there, too. He was certain she'd said she was babysitting this morning. Given the way she was gawking at Eli, he had a hunch the boy had something to do with her changed plans. He grimaced. He'd have to find a way to keep some distance between them. He did not want Giselle falling for any boy. Not yet.

"Don't look so grim," Alicia murmured. "Eli's a great kid. Besides, they're only becoming friends."

"Uh-huh." He wasn't going to argue it and wreck the day, but Jack intended to keep an eye on the pair. After all, his primary goal in coming to Churchill was to protect his daughter. When he sensed Alicia was ready, he beckoned for everyone to gather round her. Then he asked, "Where do we start?"

Alicia proved Lucy correct. She did have a timetable and it didn't include standing idle. Within five minutes she had assigned everyone a job. Hector rumbled off in his old but serviceable truck while

Jack helped the boys measure the digging area. They then outlined it with orange spray paint.

Jack dug a small section to demonstrate the depth he and Alicia wanted. Later, when he glanced over his shoulder, he saw her demonstrating the way to use a wedge to split the logs to Matt and Bennie. She had a deft hand and the boys seemed eager to become just as good. Jack paused a moment to wonder where and when Alicia had acquired such skill.

That's when he noticed a few onlookers had gathered at the side of the stone house. Their focus was on Alicia. Jack was near enough to catch their rude whispers about "that Indian woman." He'd heard denigrating comments about Aboriginal people for years, but never had those comments made him so angry or caused him to understand why Alicia felt so strongly about educating others about her culture.

Alicia must have heard because she was closer to them than he, but she pretended nothing was wrong as she continued to work, smiling her encouragement at the boys, urging them to keep splitting the logs.

Jack's blood boiled when one man commented a little louder with more obnoxious bias than the others. Unable to let it pass, he turned, met the man's mocking stare and said, "I was told Churchill is a community where people work together. So where do you want to pitch in and help?"

He should have been pleased when the man

flushed a purplish red and quickly left with his pals, but all Jack felt was heartsick sorrow that this kind, generous woman who gave so much should be treated so shabbily. He wondered how often Alicia had to endure such attitudes and decided he'd now be on the lookout to quash any bias he encountered.

Then Hector reappeared with a load of driftwood logs. Alicia produced something she called an adze and showed the boys how to use it to shape split logs into planks for the floor. Every so often she had the groups rotate so that each boy had an opportunity to try their hands at every skill and no one got bored.

At noon Laurel arrived with bag lunches for everyone. Grateful for the break, Jack sat on the smooth surface of a massive boulder, closed his eyes and took a long, deep drink from his water bottle.

"Tired?" Alicia sank down beside him. In contrast to his lack of energy, she looked revitalized.

"Will you think I'm wimpy if I say yes?" Funny how much it mattered what Alicia thought of him.

She tossed her head back in a burst of laughter.

"There is no way you could ever look wimpy, Jack," she assured him.

"I feel like a dishrag. How do teachers do it?" he asked. "Twenty-five, thirty kids in their rooms, and yet most of them maintain order for an entire school year. I've got to give teachers credit."

Alicia seemed to freeze.

Her shoulders hunched as she unwrapped her sandwich and took a bite. The tension that filled the air between them was palpable.

"Good thing I never chose that profession. I like to crack the whip. Law and order's more my style," he joked, hoping to make her smile.

"Order. That's why you let Bennie dig a foot beyond the lines?" She chuckled when he jerked upright and peered at the area below them where he'd been working. "You never noticed?"

"No. I was focusing on teaching Adam to level the ditch we made," he said, tilting his head toward the youngest boy. "We'll fill it in after lunch."

"Why?" She studied him. "There's no right or wrong size here, Jack. We can make it however we want. It doesn't *have* to be square," she said, tongue in cheek. "Odd shapes are fine."

"Go ahead. Laugh at me. I'm too tired to be offended." He leaned back and let the heat of the rock penetrate his aching back.

"Why are you so tired?" she asked quietly. "We didn't do enough to wear you out this morning."

"I was up at five." He felt stupid for even admitting it. "I wanted to do some landscaping at the lodge with those stones that were piled up at the back of the lot. It was heavy work."

"Well, for goodness' sake, why add this?" Alicia glared at him. "You don't have to kill yourself. There will be plenty more to do here in coming days."

"I promised I'd help and I intend to," he insisted.

Jack didn't say that he had come because he'd wanted to spend time with her. He didn't tell her he admired the way she devoted her attention to each boy as she taught them what they needed to know. He most especially didn't say he admired *her*.

"Don't overdo it," she cautioned. "I don't want to be responsible for injuries." She pulled a paper out of her back pocket. "Would you sign my petition?"

"Petition for what?" Jack scanned the paper, noted that many of the signatures belonged to her friends who worked or helped out at Lives.

"I'm asking council to hire a presentation from an Inuit couple for the August celebration when we'll unveil the sod house."

Jack blinked. "But you just got the concession for the land for this house from them."

"I know." She flashed her gorgeous smile at him. "Strike while the iron is hot, right?" She laughed at his surprise. "If you don't push a little, you'll never get ahead." She pointed to a line on the paper. "Need a pen?"

"No. I brought my own." He pulled his pen from his shirt pocket and signed his name where she indicated. When he looked up, her dark eyes met his. He thought he saw something sparkling in their depths. "I hope you get your wish. You're quite a lady, Alicia."

"Thank you for saying that," she said quietly, in a

somber tone. "Not everyone thinks so." She glanced over one shoulder to where the obnoxious man had earlier been standing.

"You have your work cut out for you educating those who don't appreciate what your people bring to the table," Jack said, needing to show his support.

Alicia's eyes widened. "Thank you for saying that." She looked at him until a smile tinged with relief lit her eyes. After half a second Jack returned that smile, thinking that Alicia seemed able to impact everyone she came in contact with. Especially him.

Suddenly she jumped up and strode toward a tall, dark-haired man who was climbing up the smooth boulders toward them, her smile blazing.

"Rick! I'm glad you came. We're just having lunch. Want some?"

When Alicia introduced Jack to Churchill's youngest minister, she went on endlessly about Rick's wonderful qualities. It seemed forever until she finally sat down. And then she offered Rick half her lunch. Something inside Jack grew so irritated by her obvious admiration of the guy that he got up and asked Laurel to find another lunch, which he then gave to Rick.

Only when Jack sat back down did it occur to him that he was acting like a jealous man. But that was foolish. Rick was married. Besides, Alicia was nothing to Jack.

Except a friend.

Was that why he felt so protective of her? Did friendship account for the steady stream of details he noticed, like the strong, confident way she moved, the gentle touch she showered on the boys and the sweetness of her smile whenever she spoke to Giselle? Was friendship why he longed to run his fingers through her glossy hair?

When Rick and Alicia became involved in a conversation about talking to God, Jack listened in. Questions began to roll through his brain. How was it that Alicia seemed to have the whole God thing sorted and he felt as if he was walking blindfolded through his faith?

Jack moved closer, sipped his water and really listened to their conversation. Perhaps it could help him figure out what he truly believed about God. Maybe, if he was going to have faith, he had to trust when miracles like Giselle happened, and when they didn't—like Simone's death.

As Jack realized he was thinking about his faith again, he also realized this was just one more area where Alicia had impacted his world.

It was getting much harder to keep his distance, because his heart wanted to get involved with this wonderful vibrant woman, to share the highs and lows of each day with her, to look forward with her instead of looking back.

Unfortunately his head wasn't willing to take the risk.

Chapter Nine

Alicia finished the last few details of her display for the Canada Day parade. She was proud of her country and she wanted other Canadians to appreciate their land, as well. So each year she made a special effort to enter a unique float for the July First parade, hoping to interest others to learn more about their heritage.

When she'd tweaked everything to her satisfaction, Hector drove the borrowed flat wagon to the start of the parade route. Alicia hurried inside her store to change. Then she'd follow him. Judging by the people she'd seen gathered along the street, a number of tourists were present for the festivities. That would be good for business.

Now dressed in her costume, she hurried to the counter to pick up the basket of beaded bracelets she intended to toss to the kids.

"Alicia, you look amazing." Giselle stood in the

doorway, brown eyes gaping from the white circles of her clown face.

"I'll second that. Incredible even." Jack stood behind his daughter. The admiration blazing from his blue eyes made Alicia's heart pound.

"Thank you." The bells on her ankles tinkled as she bowed. The feathers on her headpiece shivered when she looked up. "But neither of you is supposed to see me until I appear in the parade," she chided with a smile.

"We just wanted to ask if we could help you with anything," Giselle murmured.

Alicia raised an eyebrow. *We?* As far as she knew, Jack had refused to get involved in the Canada Day celebrations beyond allowing Giselle to walk as a clown and hand out leaflets about the hotel. He hadn't mentioned the kite flying.

"I thought you weren't interested," she said to Jack.

"The boys couldn't find enough wood for the fire you need this afternoon, for your 'Making of the Bannock' so I asked Dad to help us." Giselle grinned at Jack.

"Nagged is more like it. And she doesn't even know what bannock is, Alicia," Jack teased. When he smiled, it did funny things to her composure.

"Do so." Giselle shot an exaggerated glare at her father. "It's a kind of flat bread indigenous North Americans made with flour, baking powder, sugar, lard and water or milk. It's baked in an oven or cooked on a stick."

"That's right," Alicia said. "First Nations people didn't always have those ingredients though, so they used whatever resources were available. Flour from trees, sap for sugar and whatever leavening agents they could find."

"You are incredible," Jack murmured. "All this history, this information—it's an amazing gift you give to people."

"Thanks." Alicia blushed at his effusive praise, wondering for just a moment what it would be like to have someone on your side all the time, to praise you when things got tough, to cheer you when you didn't think you could handle something, to defend you when trouble loomed. A loud whine broke through her musing. "There's the horn for the parade lineup. I need to go."

The peal of the phone stopped her.

But when she picked it up, that hateful voice demanded, "Where's your kid?"

Jack's eyes were on her, noticing every detail. Alicia couldn't speak, couldn't tell her caller to leave her alone. So she did the only thing she could. She hung up. Then she unplugged the phone.

"Is something wrong?" Jack asked, his eyes narrowing.

"No. But I can't take any more calls now," she

said, coming up with the excuse quickly. "I have to leave or Hector will be driving an empty float."

"I need to go, too. See you later." Giselle scurried out the door.

"This clown thing—you don't think it will be too much for her?" Jack asked. "I mean, it's hot today and she's wearing that huge suit."

"The parade route is short, Jack. She'll be fine. As long as she has enough candy to pass out. The kids here love candy."

"I think kids everywhere love candy," he said in a dry tone. "Since Giselle is pulling a wagon full of it she should be okay." He stood back to study her and shook his head. "I can't get over how you look." He indicated the basket she held. "Can I carry that for you?"

"Thanks. It's heavy," she warned. "I made a lot of these bracelets. I didn't want to run out." She had been following him to the door but when he abruptly stopped, Alicia bumped into him. "Sorry," she apologized, drawing away from the contact as quickly as she could.

It should have made her nervous that she'd brushed against him. It always had before. Yet all Alicia could think about now was the smooth softness of his chambray shirt grazing her skin. Her nostrils filled with the citrusy scent of his aftershave.

Jack was focused on something else.

"Are you telling me that you hand-made each of these bracelets?" He gaped at her.

"Yes, of course." Alicia looked down, suddenly self-conscious.

"But that's an incredible amount of effort!"

"I usually do them during the winter when it's too cold to go outside or I have nothing to do in the evenings," she explained. "It keeps me busy. I like that."

"You're always busy." He scrutinized her face. "Too busy."

"For what?" Why would he care that she kept busy? Was Jack concerned about her?

"I don't know. Something fun. I thought after you got the land for the sod house you'd celebrate with a spa day or something," he muttered.

"Good idea. Except there is no spa in Churchill, Jack." And she'd never had a spa day in her life. Hiding her smile, Alicia tilted her head to one side to look at him. "I went for a walk. Does that count?"

"I guess. You're alone a lot, aren't you?" His voice was soft, thoughtful.

"Hardly. I'm in the store every day." What was Jack getting at?

"Yes." He kept looking at her, his blue eyes searching hers. "That's not exactly what I meant. Can I ask you something?"

"Sure." Alicia checked the clock. Hector would be wondering where she was.

"Who is the person you're searching for? The adopted person," Jack clarified.

"Why do you ask?" Her breath stopped in her throat. Tension whipped a line across her shoulders. Only by sheer force did Alicia retain control.

"You seem desperate to find them." Jack shrugged. "Maybe I could help."

"Maybe you could," she agreed. "Thank you for offering. But right now I have to get to the float. Could you please give me a ride?"

Alicia didn't need a ride. She walked everywhere and loved it. But Jack was getting too close. She had to keep him busy until she could think of an excuse not to tell him her secrets.

"Sure." He jerked a thumb toward the back door. "If we go out that way, my truck's around the corner."

"Thank you." Relief filled Alicia as she snapped the lock on the front door then hurried to his truck.

Once there, she had to remove her headdress and set it on the seat between them. She appreciated Jack's helping hand as she climbed inside and his respect of her outfit when he shifted her white buckskin skirt so it wouldn't catch in the door.

One thought sang through her brain as they drove to the parade organizing point. *Not yet.* She didn't want to admit to him that she'd given away her baby yet. But Jack would keep asking unless she told him not to, and doing that would only make him more curious.

Maybe the best thing would be to avoid him and Giselle altogether.

But she liked working with Jack. Anyway, it would be impossible to avoid them when they were both working on the sod house. And now it seemed Giselle had involved him in her bannock making this afternoon. In fact, Jack was becoming a greater part of her life with every day that passed. So much so that Alicia could no longer imagine Churchill without him.

Was that a good thing?

By the time Jack found her float, Hector had already pulled into the lineup. Obviously relieved, he held out a hand to help her climb onto the deck, but in that second Alicia couldn't move. Her heart surged into her throat because she finally realized why Jack always made her so nervous.

She was starting to care for him.

Jack couldn't take his eyes off Alicia. She looked stunning and graceful and utterly compelling as she stood in the sunlight. From the rich black of the eagle feathers on her head, to the brilliant red beads holding it in place like a frame around her face, to the flow of the milky-white garments she wore, even right down to the leather moccasins on her feet, Alicia Featherstone looked every inch a beautiful Indian maiden.

When she gathered her skirts around her to climb onto the float with Hector's help, Jack stepped in front of the other man. Ignoring the questioning look on Alicia's face, he spanned his hands around her waist and lifted her up so she sat on the side of the flat deck.

"Thank you, Jack." Her voice was as lovely as the rest of her, sweet and melodic on the shimmering breeze off the bay. There were a thousand things he wanted to say and none that seemed important enough to break the current that locked their gazes.

Alicia rose in one fluid motion. She stared at him with an intensity that echoed and brought light to a dark place inside him. Then she smiled said, "See you later," and took her place beside the teepee.

Moments later the parade line started to move. Jack drove his truck into the parking space behind his hotel. Then he went to stand on Kelsey, the main street through the town, and watch with the rest of the community. For such a small place, there were a lot of floats and everyone had something to toss to the kids. Giselle appeared about halfway through, running, but most of all smiling. A burst of pride spilled inside him. She was *his* daughter. No matter who had given her life.

To Jack's surprise, an acrobat accompanied Giselle, a lithe and tall boy who excelled at handstands and flips. He was pretty sure it was Eli and that made his mouth tighten, but since the boy was helping Giselle hand out flyers and candy from his hotel, he could hardly begrudge the two of them the time together. He stayed where he was. He didn't want to miss the first glimpse of Alicia's float.

He caught his breath when he saw her. She looked so lovely, sitting next to her stone-rimmed campfire with a mounted fox and deer watching. He joined in the burst of applause that welcomed her float, insanely proud that he knew this talented woman. In fact, Jack was so focused on Alicia, he didn't see anything that followed. It was only when one of his patrons spoke to him that he realized the parade was over.

Jack went into the lodge to make lunch, but he'd barely taken out the bread for sandwiches when Giselle came rushing in and told him that everyone was gathering in an open space behind Kelsey Street.

"There are food booths there, Dad," she called from her bedroom. "Laurel has the boys cooking burgers on grills. I'm going to help them. Want to come? I think Alicia will be there after she changes."

The mention of Alicia settled it. Jack put the bread away. "Sure." He smiled when she returned, divested of the clown costume. "Aren't you tired?"

"No. Like Alicia says, the more you do, the more you want to do. Didn't you think Eli was great?" she enthused.

"Yes, he was." But it was Alicia on whom he fixated. She was changing Giselle's world, too. It seemed to Jack that no one could avoid being impacted by her.

As he and Giselle walked to the celebration area, Jack realized that he liked being part of the changes Alicia wrought. The lethargy he'd brought to Churchill had dissipated. He hadn't felt so alive in years. And that was Alicia's doing.

The open area was teeming with kids of all ages. He wondered what they seemed to be waiting for, and was about to find Laurel and ask when the volunteer firemen turned their hoses on. In seconds the huge area was covered with billowing piles of foam. Screaming with delight, the kids dashed into it until they were covered. Then they tossed the foam around, filling the square with laughter.

"It's not toxic," Alicia said in his ear. "They take special precautions about that. Want to try?"

Her grin dared him, so Jack grabbed a handful and plopped it on her head. Laughing and trying to dodge his outstretched hand, she darted into the foam and emerged covered from jeans to T-shirt in white fluffy globs. Her hands were full of the stuff and she proceeded to dab it all over his chin.

It might seem somewhat juvenile to someone who wasn't familiar with Churchill, Jack thought as he glanced around, but it seemed that everyone in town was joining in the fun. Casting off his inhibitions, he joined her, scooping a handful of foam and placing a perfect peak of white on her nose. Alicia ducked away, laughing as she moved forward again and piled foam on his head.

"Oh, no you don't." Jack grabbed her arm to stop her.

Instantly Alicia froze. For a second her eyes showed pure terror. With a fierce intensity she said, "No!" Then she jerked away.

Something was definitely wrong. Jack dropped his hand and stood still, waiting till she fought off whatever it was. It was clear to him that something had happened to her. He'd seen that look before— the look of abject terror that victims wore.

"It's okay," he said, choosing his words with care. "I was only teasing, Alicia."

To her credit she snapped back immediately.

"I know that." She forced a smile to her lips, but her face was pale. Too pale. "Sorry. Something happened to me once, a while ago and—"

"I understand," Jack interrupted. He didn't want her to say more, didn't want her to have to rehash it all when the effect was so obviously negative. "Would you like to get some lunch?"

A hamburger was the last thing Jack wanted right now. What he did want shocked him. He wanted to enfold Alicia in his arms, to protect her and reassure her that nothing would ever hurt her again.

But that wasn't going to happen. He could see her

visibly withdrawing, pulling that mantle of protection around her.

So she wouldn't need anyone?

Or so she wouldn't need him?

"I am hungry," she murmured, and mustered a smile. "I missed breakfast. A hamburger sounds good."

"Okay. I'm buying. Let's support the Lives' barbecue." He walked with her to the stand where Rod took their order. By mutual unspoken agreement, they carried their food to the cliffs. Once there Alicia chose a sunny spot on a huge boulder and sank down cross-legged.

"I wish I could do that," he murmured. "You're very agile."

"It's in my blood, I guess. My people have been sitting like this for years." Normally when Alicia spoke about her heritage there was a thread of pride underlying them. But these words came out flat.

"Someone hurt you badly, didn't they?" Jack asked, risking a rebuff because somehow he needed to help her.

"Yes." That, too, sounded flat, devoid of feeling.

"I won't ever do that, Alicia." He waited a long time for her to look at him.

"I know," she said very softly. Then she smiled. It was like seeing the sunshine after days of dreary dark clouds. "Let's eat."

Hoping to lift her mood, Jack asked questions about the day's events.

"First there will be a pull contest." She chuckled at his quizzical look. "It's a contest to see who can pull the heaviest load. In the old days there were very few horses that made it to Churchill. You were wealthy if you had sled dogs to pull your supplies in the winter. If you didn't, you did it yourself."

"How?" Jack thought he could watch her face forever. It was like a big screen, expressing her inner thoughts with its ever-changing mobility.

"Well, you could've made a kind of sled and fit it with a harness that you then put on and pulled your supplies home." She chewed a French fry for a moment. "That's kind of what they do for the adults. It's loaded with flour or something. There's a prize for the one who pulls the most weight. The kids participate, too."

"They pull flour, too?"

"No, silly." She laughed at him and, to Jack's amazement, he didn't mind a bit. "They pull quads. Some people call them four-wheelers or all-terrain vehicles," she clarified. "Smaller ones for the little kids."

"And after that?" This was going to be a Canada Day very different from those he'd spent in Vancouver.

"Lots of races for kids and adults. And, of course, the kite flying." She winked at him.

"You had to say it, didn't you? I'd almost forgotten." He sighed.

"I'll cheer you and Giselle on," Alicia promised, flashing another of those teasing grins.

"That's it?" He wanted to spend more of the day with her. Probably not the best idea given that he didn't want to get involved, but Jack didn't stop to reason that out.

"There's a sand castle building contest on the beach. Some people go swimming." She nodded when he shivered. "The Bay never really gets warm, I'm afraid. The rest of the day is mostly visiting, walking around, touring the museum—just enjoying the community."

"And your bannock," he added. "But I heard there'd be a bonfire." His skin reacted with a tingle when he thought about sharing an evening bonfire with Alicia. Even with the town gathered, Jack felt certain it would seem more intimate than those they'd shared at Lives with the boys.

"There is a bonfire. It gets started around nine but most people show up closer to eleven, because the sun stays up so long these days." Alicia leaned her arms behind her, tipped her head back and lifted her face to the sunshine. "Some people roast wieners or marshmallows, but you have to bring your own supplies. And a warm jacket. It can be cool."

"I see." Jack couldn't take his eyes off her.

"Do you?" She twisted to look directly at him.

"It's nothing fancy, Jack. It's just the way this community, with family and friends, celebrates the freedom we have in our country."

"I think it's great," he said, and he meant it. He spared a moment to think about the past and the times he'd left Simone and Giselle to celebrate alone while he focused on work. If he'd learned nothing else from Simone's death, he'd learned that family was everything. That's why he'd moved to Churchill.

They talked about a lot of things—the sod house, Alicia's schedule for it, her plans for the future. Then she turned the tables. Jack skirted around her questions about finding Giselle's birth mother because he didn't want to dampen their time together with his problems. He wanted to enjoy his time with Alicia this afternoon. He wanted that a lot.

When he was finally alone tonight, Jack knew he was going to have to examine that want more deeply. Liking Alicia was one thing. Getting romantically involved with her? That couldn't happen, especially now because he realized just how bereft his world would be without Alicia in it. He was getting too close.

He kept her company during the kids' races on the main drag, surprised that she'd helped the Lives' boys organize and enter a team. The two of them stood on the sidelines, shouting their encouragement, giddy with laughter when their group edged out the competition by a fraction.

Alicia was thrilled at the boys' prize of three hundred dollars. She was so excited Jack struggled to keep his balance when she threw her arms around him. Just as quickly she pulled away, her face flushed, her eyes avoiding his. To spare her, he pretended nothing was amiss but was secretly delighted that she was able to lose herself with him.

Later he built the fire she needed to cook her bannock on sticks. People gathered around, enjoying the Native food and asking her questions. Alicia was in her element, freely sharing with anyone. Hot and flushed, two hours later he finally persuaded her to take a break to cool off with the soda he brought her. Alicia was thrilled that her efforts had been so appreciated. Jack had never admired anyone so much.

When darkness fell and the only thing he could see was her face in the flickering firelight, when his shoulder rubbed hers as the group sang "O Canada," Jack began to wonder if it might be different this time, if it would be worth the risk to love again.

Dare he embrace these feelings for Alicia that had taken root? Dare he trust God not to let him lose again?

At first thought, the risk seemed too great. But walking Alicia home after the fire, brushing a kiss against her cheek and squeezing her hand in a gentle touch that she returned—all of these caused a persuasive yearning that left Jack sitting on his back deck far into the night, searching for trust.

Chapter Ten

Alicia swiped a hand across her perspiring forehead as she mopped up the last of the water the next day. This was not her plan for Sunday.

She carried the bucket outside to dump the dingy water on her straggling flowers and nearly yelped to find Jack standing there. Immediately her heart started its rapid rat-a-tat. But Jack didn't look as he had last time she'd seen him. Now his blue eyes were cloudy and his mouth didn't stretch in that persuasive smile.

"Have you been doing this all day?" he asked.

"It seems like it." She sighed. "The sink downstairs has a leak. By the time I came from church it had flooded everything. I finally figured out how to shut it off. I've been cleaning up all afternoon. This is the last of the water, I hope."

The tension around his eyes eased somewhat. "I wondered why you didn't show."

"Show?" She narrowed her eyes, trying to decipher his meaning.

"We had a meeting." He frowned. "You forgot? I didn't think there was anything about that sod house project that you'd forget."

"Jack, I don't recall promising to be at any meeting," she said.

"Technically, I guess you didn't agree. Laurel said she wanted to get us all together to discuss safety after Daniel cut himself with the adze. You weren't around and Eli was busy with a customer, so I left you a note right beside that reed bowl on the counter."

"I haven't seen any note. Come on in." Mystified, she led the way back inside, dropping her bucket in the corner before she sifted through the pile of papers she hoped to sort through with Lucy tomorrow morning.

A letter she'd received from the adoption agency sat on top. Though Alicia tried to cover it, it was clear Jack had seen it.

"That's the agency I'm trying to get to unseal Giselle's documents," Jack said. "That friend you're helping—was he or she adopted from there?"

"Friend?" She blanked for a second. "Oh. Yes," she said, realizing that he thought her lost child was a former friend.

"Maybe we could work together, help each other," Jack offered.

"It's very nice of you, but the agency says they have no information for me." She tucked the letter under the counter. "I don't see your note."

"Here." He lifted it out of the basket. "Someone must have put it inside by mistake."

That "someone" was her. Unable to read the scrawl, Alicia had assumed Eli was using the sheet to work out a tag for an article. She shook her head when Jack flipped it open to show her where he'd penciled her name.

"Oh, for goodness' sake. I had no idea." She lifted her head and smiled into his lovely blue eyes. "You're right. I wouldn't have missed the meeting if I'd known. I'm sorry, Jack."

"Doesn't matter. I'm sure you know all about safety." He shrugged. "Laurel just wanted to remind the boys to be careful around those sharp tools. She thought you'd want to be there. You are our fearless leader, after all." He grinned.

She blushed and dipped her head, pleased but a little off balance at the way her heart bumped whenever he flashed that smile at her. She began to wring out the old towels she'd used to mop up the floor.

"That's nice of you, though untrue. It's a group effort."

To her surprise Jack pitched in right alongside to help her clean up what was left, even though she tried to dissuade him. It was a bit disconcerting to have him so near. Alicia struggled to keep the conversation flowing.

"It's going well, don't you think? The sod house, I mean." She turned, surprised to find his face inches from hers. "We should have a special celebration for the kids after our grand opening," she quickly said to cover the confusion Jack always caused her.

"Great idea." Jack carried the basket with the cloths to the washer, threw the towels inside, then leaned one hip against the dryer as he waited for her to start the machine. "Since you've been doing drudgery all afternoon, what would you say to a walk?"

"Yes." She smiled. Nothing sounded better than more time with Jack. "Just let me change."

"There's nothing wrong with what you're wearing, Alicia," he said, casting an eye over her jeans and old red T-shirt. "You look cute, especially with your hair in pigtails."

"But my jeans have holes in the knees." She wished she didn't always feel so awkward around him.

"Haven't you heard?" Jack looped an arm around her shoulders and drew her outside with him. "Holes in the knees are very fashionable lately."

Alicia was pretty sure he was joking, but she couldn't resist his smile or his friendly touch and before she knew it they were strolling down the path to the beach.

"Oh, the boys are here," she said, delighted when they ran over to greet her.

The boys told them Laurel had built a fire for a hot dog cookout.

"Why don't you join us? Plenty for all," Laurel said. But Alicia noticed the woman raised an eyebrow as she glanced at her brother's arm around Alicia's shoulders.

Alicia ducked away, embarrassed to admit how much she enjoyed his touch.

Giselle, along with Kyle and Sara Loness, Laurel's employees, were also at the beach. While Sara held their baby, Kyle showed the boys how to get in and out of the dingy he'd brought. Alicia took a turn holding the baby and sharing local gossip with Sara until a pack of hungry boys begged Laurel to start their supper early. Adam flopped down on the rock beside Alicia.

"My dad says Indians are no good," he said in a belligerent tone.

Alicia happened to be looking at Jack and saw the chagrin alter his face. She was embarrassed he'd heard those words, but she would not back down.

"Does he?" she said. "I think perhaps he doesn't know us or the history of Canada. Did you know Native Canadians lived in this land for hundreds of years before Europeans arrived?"

Aware that the other boys had gathered around, she talked of how different tribes hunted and fished, the way they took care of the land so as to leave a legacy for their grandchildren.

"But the land was taken. The treaties Indians made with white men were broken. Right, Alicia?" Eli said.

"Yes, the treaties were broken on both sides. Many of the reservations were unlike the land Native Canadians were used to. Animals they'd lived on, like the buffalo, were decimated," she told them. "Men and boys could no longer roam freely to hunt. They lived in impoverished conditions, often isolated and ill."

Alicia paused, glanced around. Jack's eyes met hers, dark navy and glowing. He smiled and nodded, as if to encourage her.

"But despite disease and terrible conditions, Native Canadians survived and are now contributing members to society. My people have a rich culture and heritage. There is much we can learn from the old ways, just as we always gain knowledge when we accept other cultures and the people in them."

Adam was silent for a long time. Then he looked up and grinned at her.

"If my dad says it again, I'm going to tell him to try some bannock on a stick with your blueberry preserve. You could sell that for a lot of money."

"I already do." Alicia winked at him and the group burst into laughter.

The others straggled away to roast another hot

dog. Adam lingered then finally bent to look her in the eye.

"I'm sorry I said that, Alicia. I don't think my dad even knows any Indians personally. I wish he could meet you. You make knowing about Indians so interesting."

"Because we are." Alicia touched his shoulder. "Just because someone is different from us isn't a good enough reason to diss them," she murmured quietly so none of the others would hear.

"I'll remember that." Adam smiled then hurried to join the boys in a game of beach volleyball.

"Nicely done," Jack murmured in her ear. He handed her a hot dog covered with relish, onions and mustard. "You're a born teacher, Alicia."

She'd been sailing high until Jack had said "teacher." Immediately thoughts of Mr. Parcet invaded.

"You're not eating your hot dog," Jack said disapprovingly.

"I'm not fond of mustard," she murmured, trying to cover her discomfort. She hadn't expected he'd tug the hot dog out of her hand. "It's not a big deal."

"Yes, Alicia, it is. Why should you eat something you don't care for?" Jack held out the hot dog he'd given her. "See, I happen to love mustard." He took a giant bite. "Why don't you prepare your own hot dog the way you like it?"

So she did. Then she joined in a game of tag, let

the boys try to teach her the basics of volleyball and flew Giselle's kite, the one Alicia had repaired after Jack had crashed it on Canada Day. When the bright red-and-white maple leaf was soaring above the bay she handed it over to Jack.

"But I don't know what to do," he protested.

"That's the thing, Jack. You don't *do* anything." She rested her hands on his to demonstrate. "Feel that? It's the wind pulling. Let it. Just gently guide where it goes."

"I'm not sure—"

She eased her hands off his. Not because she didn't like holding his hands but because she wanted to hold them tighter and she didn't think he'd like that.

"Sometimes I think flying a kite gives us perspective on how God works," she said.

"Meaning?" Jack chanced a look at her before he returned his scrutiny to the kite.

"A little nudge here, a poke there, a gust of wind to straighten us out when we get off track." She encouraged him to let out more string. "It's only when we, like the kite, try to take control and go our own way that we get into trouble."

"Trust in the master kite-flyer, is that what you're saying?" he said, giving her a droll look.

"That is what I'm saying," she said firmly. "Because He's the one who knows the wind currents and sideswipes life will bring."

"I envy you your faith, Alicia."

"Why? Don't you have the same?" she asked, surprised when he handed the kite back to her.

"No," he admitted. "But I think maybe it's time I tried to emulate yours. Could we go back to your place to discuss something? I need your help."

Alicia nodded. She reeled in the kite and gave it back to Giselle, who asked her dad's permission to return to Lives with the boys to play some board games.

"Sure," Jack told her. He glanced at his sister. "If it's all right with your aunt." Laurel nodded. "I'll pick you up in—"

"A couple of hours?" Laurel said. She hugged Alicia. "Thanks for not taking offense with Adam and teaching him. I know his words hurt."

"I'm glad if I helped him." Alicia hugged her back, then watched the group drive away.

"You're sure you don't mind listening to my troubles for a while?" Jack asked when they were alone on the beach.

"What are friends for?" Alicia asked.

But as they walked up the hill and across the street to her place, she knew she wanted a lot more than friendship from Jack. The thing was, she felt nervous and skittish around him, like a schoolgirl on her first date with the most incredible guy.

Which, technically, she was.

Lord? Help!

* * *

"Come on in. Welcome."

The first thing that struck Jack as he entered Alicia's upstairs apartment was that it felt like home. There was nothing showy or chic about it. In fact, the plaid sofa looked well used and comfortable, as did an overstuffed chair with a knitted throw on its back. A table with two chairs sat in front of the worn but spotless kitchen. On the table was a glass bottle with a few wildflowers Jack had seen growing on the bluffs. Everything in the place spoke to him of nature—shades of brown, taupe, yellow, with hints of red blended in a peaceful backdrop for her beauty.

Her place was plain, ordinary and, yet, he felt welcome here.

"Would you like some coffee?" she asked, obviously on edge.

"What I'd really love is a glass of water," he told her with a smile. "I can still taste all that mustard."

After a startled look at him, Alicia laughed, poured the water and handed it to him. She sat down in the big chair. Jack had a hunch she sat there often. Her Bible lay open on a table beside it.

"Is something wrong?" she asked him.

"Yes." Jack drank the water in one gulp. "It's about Giselle. She's insistent that she meet her birth mother."

Alicia's eyes widened. "You've found her?"

"Not yet. But I've found out some troubling things about her." He sucked in a breath, hating to say the words because that would somehow make them real. "As I told you, there's only a little information and that covers the two years after Giselle's birth. After that there's nothing, at least nothing I can uncover."

"Only two years?" Alicia's dark eyes fixed on something unseen. She gnawed on her bottom lip for a few moments before looking directly at him. "Tell me what you're worried about."

"I'm worried she might have lived on the street." The way she stared at him told Jack Alicia was thinking along the same lines. "How can I tell Giselle that?"

"I don't know, but I think you have to tell her the truth or she's going to make up her own truth. In fact, she's already doing it." Alicia sighed. "Maybe you don't realize this, Jack, but Giselle now sees herself as partly Native Canadian. She's comparing herself with me and glamorizing my life into some kind of fairy-tale dream. It's utterly unrealistic."

"Because she wants to be like you," Jack said, recognizing the truth.

"I don't believe she understands who I am." Alicia frowned, trying to figure out a way to make him comprehend. "She's got this idealized image in her head, like a movie character that sails above life's problems and biases."

"I know." Jack made a face. "When she was little she used to watch a video called *Pocahontas*. She watched it over and over. We probably fed into her fantasy by giving her an Indian maiden outfit for dress up." He felt like an idiot saying this in front of a woman who'd struggled with her Native identity. "Neither I nor Simone knew a thing about your culture."

"Jack." Alicia smiled as she touched his arm with the tips of her fingers. "You don't owe me any explanation."

"No." But that didn't stop the memories from washing back like a tidal wave. "Simone was a great mother. She got into the spirit of the thing with Giselle, chasing her, playing bow and arrows in the backyard."

"Tell me about Simone, Jack." Alicia's soft voice drew him in, reassuring, comforting.

It had been so long since he'd talked about her, shared the details of his loss. For a moment he got lost in reminiscing. With that came wrenching, gutting pain. They'd been solid, together, a family. Could he be that for Giselle now? It seemed impossible.

"Tell me," she prodded.

"Are you sure?" He smiled with self-mockery. "Sometimes I think I talk about her too much."

"You can tell me anything," Alicia said. "Just let yourself talk."

So he did. He told her how lucky he'd felt to be Simone's husband, how beautiful she was and how she seemed to do everything with style and grace. But as he talked, Jack realized that the memories that had once caused pain had now lost their sting. He also realized he was beginning to forget her voice, her perfume, her laugh. That bothered him so much he let his voice trail away. When he looked back to Alicia he found her studying him, a faint frown on her lips.

"I'm sorry," he muttered. "I've talked too long."

"Not at all. It's clear that you loved your wife very much." She paused. "It's just—"

"Yes?" He waited, puzzled by her hesitation yet sensing she had something important she needed to say. "What?"

"I don't want to hurt you, Jack. I'd never want that." Alicia cleared her throat. "But the way you talk about Simone, it's clear you idealized her. Maybe that's why Giselle is so determined to meet her birth mother—perhaps she's afraid she could never meet the high standard you've painted of Simone."

Jack felt a twinge of irritation. Simone *had* been amazing. He checked his emotion. After all, Alicia was only trying to help.

"Maybe the reason Giselle is so anxious about her birth mother is because Simone wouldn't tell her the truth, because she kept the adoption a secret." Alicia bit her lip, then spoke the words that had obviously been festering inside her. "I'm guessing that your daughter thinks Simone was embarrassed or ashamed of Giselle's past."

Jack stared at her. "We would never—"

"I know," Alicia rushed to reassure him. "But that wouldn't stop her from thinking it, from wondering if she has something to be ashamed of, if she needs to prove herself."

A million little pieces of the puzzle called Giselle began to come together. Tidbits of things she'd said recently, comments she'd made about Native Canadians and their rights. Did she think she would have to defend herself because she was of Native ancestry? He'd seen the self-doubt creep into his usually confident daughter.

"I don't know what to do for her, how to help her," he said, feeling powerless.

"Giselle's strong, Jack. Stronger than you realize. Tell her the truth. Get it all in the open." Alicia's fingers gently threaded through his. "Your daughter will be fine as long as she knows she's loved. The rest is just background. Teach her that who she is depends more on what she makes of her life than where she came from."

Jack absorbed it, nodding slowly as the sense of Alicia's words sank in. But after several moments he glanced at their hands. Cradling hers between his, he stared into her eyes.

"How do you know all this, Alicia? You've never raised a child and yet you seem to have all the answers."

Her laughter chased the intensity of the moment away. She drew her hands from his, but Jack saw something fleeting dance through her eyes.

"I don't have all the answers," she assured him. "I just know God and He does. Being Indian forces you to face the facts of life and come to terms with the way things are and the way you want them to be. Being a believer means you depend on God, not yourself. When I need help, I pray for direction and then I work on helping others. That always makes me feel better."

"Maybe I need to try that more," he said.

"Maybe you do." Alicia lifted one eyebrow meaningfully and asked, "Does Giselle have any grandparents?"

"Simone's parents still live in Vancouver," he admitted quietly. "Giselle will visit them before the summer's over."

"You won't go with her?" Alicia frowned when he shook his head.

"They blame me for Simone's death," Jack explained. "Simone was investigating police corruption. The investigation didn't end with her death. I've been ordered to keep silent about the details.

Her parents think my silence means I'm to blame for her death."

Though he tried to mask the hurt of being misjudged, he knew Alicia understood.

"I'm so sorry," she whispered. "What a terrible position to be left in."

"It's fine." He shrugged it away. "As long as they love and care for Giselle, I'm okay with whatever they feel about me."

His cell phone rang a special sequence of notes that meant Giselle had texted him. He checked the message and quickly rose.

"I have to pick up Giselle at Laurel's," he said. Alicia followed him down the stairs and let him out the door.

"Drive carefully. And tell Giselle the truth," she added. "It might ease her worries to know that you haven't given up, that you're still trying to find her birth mom."

"You're always helping me, Alicia," he said quietly, peering into her lovely face. "When will you let me help you?" It was like a need deep inside him.

Quietly she said, "You already have. Good night."

Jack walked a few steps, then turned to face her.

"I'll think about what you've said," he promised.

But all he could think about on the drive to Lives was that Alicia had the most glorious dark hair, shiny brown eyes and the gentlest touch he'd ever known.

Too bad Alicia hadn't been Giselle's birth mom. She was exactly the kind of woman he wanted for his daughter.

And for himself?

Chapter Eleven

"Have you heard a word I've said about these accounts?" Lucy Clow demanded.

Alicia shook her head and offered a rueful smile. "Sorry."

"It doesn't matter. I was only explaining that Tansi is running so well, your loans should be paid off well before the five years you'd planned." Lucy closed the ledger and laid her hands on top. "Tell me what's bothering you, Alicia. I promise I won't judge."

It was so tempting to unload. Lucy had the same personality as her friend Nancy—strong, supportive but with a touch of kick start that wouldn't let you brood. Lucy was her friend. She'd been nothing but help from the first day she'd arrived. But—

"You need to talk to someone, dear. You can't remain an island forever." Lucy tilted Alicia's chin so she could look into her eyes. "Have I ever told anyone your business?"

"No. For which I thank you greatly." Alicia sighed. "It's just that I'm very confused right now. I guess I need time to sort myself out."

"What are you confused about? Or should I say whom?" Lucy smiled. "Jack?"

"He's such a nice guy. Truthful, honest, strong for his daughter." It was those very traits that made it impossible for Alicia to tell him about the rape she'd endured, and her son.

Jack the lawman would judge her for not reporting Mr. Parcet so that no other woman would be hurt. Truthfully, Alicia wished she had done that. For years she'd wondered if her silence had caused another innocent girl to be hurt.

But it was too late now. Even if she did tell her story, who would believe her after all this time? She had no proof. Mr. Parcet would deny it and in doing so make her look foolish. All she could do now was to keep her secret and figure out how to find her child.

And figure out how to rein in her growing fondness for Jack.

"Jack Campbell is a nice guy, as you say." Lucy held her gaze. "But since that talk you had with him two weeks ago, I've watched you push him away, keep him at arm's length. I don't think he means you harm, Alicia."

"No, I know that." Alicia sighed. It wasn't Jack

that had her worried. She'd had another phone call from Mr. Parcet and it was much worse than the first. He'd threatened to spread rumors about her if she didn't tell him her son's whereabouts. And he'd laughed at her threat to reveal what he'd done.

Who do you think will believe your word against mine? I'm a respected member of the community. I've sat on boards, volunteered time and donated money. My family has status and power. You don't even have a family.

How that had hurt, because she *didn't* have a family. In fact, she didn't have anyone she could ask to help her stand up against Mr. Parcet, at least nobody with the kind of power and public voice he had.

I wonder what your friends would think if they knew you'd had a kid and given him away. You threaten me, but the only proof you have, Alicia, is that kid and I'm beginning to wonder if you even know where he is. I don't expect you were a model mother.

But she'd wanted to be! How she'd wanted to love and care for and protect her child. But, at fifteen, it had been impossible.

Nobody in that town will let you near their kids if I tell them how you lived on the street.

Mr. Parcet could stop her from working with the Lives' boys! Rather than argue with her attacker, she'd hung up, firm in her determination not to tell him anything about her lead on the adoption agency. But his threat had hit home. She couldn't let Jack or Giselle, Lucy or Pastor Rick be touched by the scandal.

She especially didn't want Laurel's Lives Under Construction project damaged by negative association with her. The boys were almost finished the log house.

"Alicia?" Lucy touched her shoulder, pulling her from her thoughts. "Please tell me what's wrong?"

"I just need to manage things on my own." She smiled and hugged Lucy's frail shoulders. "That's what I've always done."

"That's why you can't read," Lucy said, her blue eyes piercing right through Alicia's.

Alicia stared at her, aghast that she'd said the words aloud.

"I taught many people to read while we were missionaries. You'd be a very quick study," Lucy coaxed. "You're smart. You could learn. Let me help you."

"I—I don't know."

For one tantalizing moment she considered it. She could do nothing about the rape, or her child or Mr. Parcet. But maybe she could change this. To be rid of the weight of it, to be able to stop making excuses, hiding the horrible secret, feeling confused and vulnerable...

"Are you sure you wouldn't mind?" she asked. Tears welled in her eyes as Lucy embraced her, assuring her that nothing would give her greater pleasure.

"We'll start tonight," Lucy whispered as the bell above the front door tingled. "I'll pray God will help you, Alicia. It'll be our secret."

"Something wrong?" Jack walked across the room and stood in front of the counter, his eyes shifting warily from Alicia to Lucy and back again. "Should I come back later?"

"No, of course not." Alicia chuckled as she surreptitiously dabbed at her tears. "I was supposed to be at the site by now, wasn't I?" she asked. He nodded.

"But if you can't make it, there's no problem. Hector's helping us cut sod. When we run out of that we'll make mud. You don't have to be there."

"I want to be. Making mud pies is the best part," she teased. She bent and kissed Lucy's cheek. "Thank you," she whispered. Then she asked aloud, "Will you be okay if I leave for a while?"

"Of course. Get away with you now, the pair of you," Lucy ordered. "People have been asking lots of questions about your project. You're going to have plenty of visitors on opening day so you'd better be finished with that house on time."

"We will be." Jack's voice blended with Alicia's in

unanimous affirmation. They looked at each other and laughed.

For the first time in a very long time, Alicia's shoulders felt lighter, as if a tiny bit of the cloud she always felt looming over her had blown away. This morning Lucy had read her another letter from the adoption agency. They refused to answer any more of Alicia's questions. Her only hope now was that somehow God would lead her to the child she'd never heard call her "Mom."

With new resolve Alicia walked through the door Jack held for her and she experienced a tiny flutter of satisfaction as they headed toward the site together. How proud she felt to have him in her life, even if she couldn't act on these growing feelings for him.

It was going to be hard to keep him at arm's length until the sod house opening, but she had to do it. For his sake and Giselle's. It was the only way to protect them from the ugliness of Mr. Parcet.

"I'm providing lunch today, did you know?" Jack made a face at Alicia's surprised look. "Hey, I can cook. Sort of."

"I'm sure it will be delicious." She pretended repentance but couldn't carry it off, and that made him laugh.

"Hamburgers on the grill are always delicious." He tossed her a cocky look. "Especially when I put on my secret sauce."

"Ketchup?" she guessed, chuckling when he couldn't hide his chagrin.

"Who talked?" Jack rolled his eyes when Alicia made a zipping motion across her lips. How he loved it when she relaxed enough to tease and make fun of him.

Jack was so drawn to Alicia, and yet, some warning in his brain told him she was hiding something. If not hiding, withholding. It made him uneasy.

They made good progress on the sod, but slapping mud on the walls was very messy. So messy that Alicia insisted that since it was such a warm day, they should wash off in the bay before lunch. Alicia raced the boys and Giselle to the bay while he got things ready for lunch. Jack had barely put on the burgers when his phone rang. He answered, listened, then hung up with a moan.

When Alicia returned she took one look at his face and asked, "What's wrong?"

Jack made a motion to wait until he served everyone and they were seated at the picnic tables he'd placed to one side of the hotel. After she'd said grace he finally sat down beside her, the smallest, most charred burger on his plate. Didn't matter. He wasn't hungry now anyway.

"Are you sick?" Alicia asked him.

"No."

"I would be if I had to eat that." With quick economical movements she divided her burger and handed him one half. "Here." When he didn't take it, she set it down on his plate, placed her elbows on the table and cupped her chin in them. "Spill it, Jack."

"You are a very bossy woman," he said.

One of the boys asked her something and she answered, but her stare on Jack never wavered. Finally he gave in.

"I have a mother and two daughters who clean rooms for me. All three of them are sick with some virus and can't come in to work," he explained. "I can't imagine how we're going to be ready when the train comes in tomorrow morning. I'm fully booked. Giselle and I will have to opt out of your fireside story at Lives tonight, I'm afraid."

"You can't miss tonight's story," Alicia told him. "It's especially for Giselle. Anyway, you won't have to."

"But—"

"We'll chip in and help you." Without pausing, she rose, got the boys' attention and told them what had happened. "Are you up for giving Jack a hand?"

They agreed immediately.

"Great. Now go get your ice-cream treats from the coffee shop. Tell them I'll be in to pay later." As they rushed away, Giselle leading the pack, Alicia sat down, picked up her half burger and grinned at him. "Issue resolved."

Jack couldn't believe it.

"Alicia, it's very hard work. You have your own business. You have to pay someone to stay at Tansi while you work on the sod house. I don't think you need another expense." He expected her to back out, but Alicia only smiled. "What?"

"Do you think Lucy would let me in the door if she knew I'd walked away from helping you?" she asked. "Anyway, I want to. Churchill is built on community. You need a helping hand so we'll help. You helped me with my water cleanup." She stole three chips off his plate and munched contentedly. "Now eat your lunch before that herd comes back."

"You're quite a lady, Alicia Featherstone," Jack said in wonder.

"I guess that's better than being called bossy." She winked at him, laughter shining in her eyes. Finished, she rose, tossed out her paper plate and began clearing the tables. "You'll have to show me what to do, Jack."

"My pleasure."

Any hesitation he felt vanished later that afternoon as Alicia slogged alongside the boys, turning the hotel into a welcoming home-away-from-home with freshly made beds, clean towels and sparkling bathrooms. Even the breakfast room was tidied and restocked. All he'd have to do in the morning was make coffee and set out the trays of food.

After they were finished, Laurel picked up the boys and Giselle and took them to swim in the pool at the community center. Alicia tossed the cleaning cloths into the laundry. After one last glance around the immaculate foyer, she fluttered her fingers.

"Gotta go," she said. "See you later."

"How about I take you to dinner? As a small token of my very great appreciation," Jack said, amazed that she could look so good after so much hard work. "Please? I hate eating alone."

She took a long time to decide but finally, peeking through her lashes at him, she nodded.

"Is The Seaview okay?" he asked, thinking perhaps she wouldn't want to go to the fanciest restaurant in town. "I'll pick you up at six."

Again she paused to think it over before nodding. "I wouldn't mind if we went to Common Grounds. It's not as expensive and—"

"They don't do steaks," Jack said. "After today I deserve a steak. So do you."

"Whatever you chose will be fine," she said. "I'd better go."

"Thank you for all your help." He tilted his head to one side as he considered the day. "You never seem to stop giving, Alicia. I admire that very much. But sometimes I wonder who gives to you."

"Everybody," she said with a smile. "Including you. You have no idea how much you've given me, Jack." Then she hurried off down the street.

He watched her duck into the coffee shop to pay

for the kids' treats. A moment later she was hurrying into Tansi, as if it were a shelter. Or a refuge.

There was so much he didn't know, didn't understand about her. And he wanted to.

Jack went inside and called Pastor Rick. He'd put this off long enough. Tomorrow, if Rick could accommodate him, he was going to make a dent in figuring out the whole faith-through-unanswered-prayer thing.

There were a thousand reasons Jack couldn't allow his feelings for Alicia. Not the least of these was the issue of faith. Alicia's was rock solid. His wasn't. More than that, Jack still couldn't forget that when he'd needed God most, he'd been abandoned. Going through it all a second time was a no-brainer. Alicia couldn't be more than a friend.

But oh, the thought of sharing Alicia's very full world tantalized him.

Alicia glanced around the room of Churchill's fanciest restaurant and felt totally out of place. Lucy had said her black slacks, turquoise top and beaded jacket were perfect for a dinner date, though of course this wasn't a date.

Lucy had also coached her on the menu so it had been easy to pretend to study the offerings and ask for something she could truly enjoy. What Lucy hadn't done was suggest a list of topics to talk to Jack about. Now the silence stretched between them, making Alicia more uncomfortable. She sipped her water.

"So what's the fireside story tonight about?" Jack asked.

"An Indian warrior who set out by canoe at night to meet his betrothed," she told him. It was her favorite Cree legend, mostly because it was full of romance and she had so little in her life. Of course, it was just a legend.

"That's a story?" Jack didn't look impressed. Their food arrived, causing a pause in the conversation. "There must be more to it," he coaxed when the waiter left.

"If I tell you, you'll be bored later," she argued.

"Bored with you? Hardly. Come on, tell me."

So in between bites of delicious fish, Alicia explained that as the Indian brave paddled in the darkness he heard the river singing and saw his favorite stars lighting his way.

"All his thoughts were of her," she murmured, aware that her story was bringing a certain intimacy to the meal. "Suddenly he heard his name called out. Puzzled, he let the canoe drift as he searched for the speaker. But he saw no one. So he called out in his native language which was Cree, *'Kâ-têpwêt?'* But no one answered."

"A scary story?" Jack murmured, eyebrows raised. "Go on."

"The brave thought he'd imagined the voice because no one answered him. So he took up his paddle and continued down the dark, murmuring river. A few moments later he heard his name called again. It came from everywhere, and from nowhere. Something about the sound reminded the brave of his beloved, but he knew she couldn't be here, along the river, because she lived many miles away." Alicia paused, saw the interest flickering in Jack's eyes. How nice it would be if this *were* a date.

"Is that it?" Jack asked, interrupting her fantasy.

"Patience," she said with a smile. "The brave knew it wasn't her, but just to be certain he asked again in his native language, 'Who calls?' And then he repeated in French, *'Qu'appelle?'* The call echoed in the surrounding valley, reverberated back to him then faded away."

"This is going to sound great in the darkness around the fire," Jack said. "You're an amazing storyteller, Alicia."

"You haven't heard it all yet." This was her favorite part of the legend. Alicia laid her utensils down and learned forward, dropping her voice. "Though the brave listened intently, he heard no response. But the breeze swirled around him, caressing his arm and his face. Almost he thought he heard his beloved whispering in his ear. Then the breeze died away. Finally the brave took up his paddle and continued his journey."

Jack sat still, his steak forgotten, his blue eyes

locked with hers. Alicia found it hard to breathe, hard to continue. But he'd wanted to hear the story and somehow now she desperately needed to finish it.

"Go on," he murmured.

"The brave arrived at dawn. His beloved's father stood on the shore. His face told the story. She was gone, had died in the night, whispering his name with her last breath. As the warrior wept he remembered the breeze touching his face and knew it had been his beloved saying goodbye. To this day, travelers on the Qu'Appelle River in Saskatchewan still hear the echo of the Cree warrior's voice as he reaches out to the spirit of his beloved, crying, '*Qu'appelle?* Who calls?'"

Partway through the last segment of the story Jack's face went as still as a mask. He let her finish speaking, then picked up his fork and cut off a piece of his steak.

"Very sweet," he said in a colorless voice.

Only then did Alicia grasp that he must be thinking of Simone, that she'd died and left him, too. All her pleasure in the evening disappeared.

She toyed with her now tasteless food, but still the silence yawned between them. She'd tell a different story for tonight, something about life and living.

"I'm sorry, Jack. I didn't mean to revive bad memories."

"That's the thing," he said slowly. "They're not

bad memories." The flicker of a smile played at the corners of his mouth. "When I think of Simone now I think of happy times, of the joy she brought to my life. I have no regrets. I was blessed to love her."

"Yes, you were," Alicia agreed as a wave of relief filled her. "Many people don't get to experience that in their lifetime."

"That's what Rick said this afternoon." Jack's tone grew thoughtful. "I'm getting a different viewpoint on a lot of things. Including God."

"I'm so glad," she whispered. One of her prayers was being answered. Jack was rebuilding his faith.

"I have to keep refocusing my thoughts." His smile was so genuine her breath caught in her throat. "God didn't run out on me, He gave me a precious gift in Simone, because He loves me. Having had that blessing in my life, Rick says I need to move on."

"Can you do that?" she asked with some trepidation.

"I have to try. I can't cling to my anger and bitterness forever." He touched her hand where it lay on the table. "Something you said keeps coming back to me."

"*I* said?" Alicia should have moved her hand away, should have suppressed the rush of delight that shivered through her when she didn't, should have kept things strictly platonic. But Jack was so amazing. How could she not enjoy these few precious moments with him?

"Yes, you," he said. Again her heart took off racing in response to Jack's piercing gaze. "You said, 'The past happened. Can't be changed. So now what are you going to do?' Do you remember saying that?"

Alicia shook her head.

"The most important part was what you said next," he murmured, his eyes moving to their clasped hands.

Finally, self-consciously, Alicia slid hers away.

"You said I only had one choice. You said I had to keep going. And you were right, Alicia." He eyes bored into hers and she could not move. "I don't understand the why of the past. Maybe I never will. But I can't waste the rest of my life being angry and frustrated."

"No, you can't," she whispered. A shaft of pain pieced her heart. The way he spoke, the softness of his voice, the quietness she sensed in him—was he going to tell her he was ready to love again? She wanted that for him. But, oh, how she wished she was the kind of woman a man like Jack could love.

"After Simone died, I vowed I'd never let myself care for anyone in that way because it left me so terribly vulnerable. I felt I could not endure losing someone who was precious to me again."

"And now you've rethought that." Alicia forced a smile.

"No," Jack said softly. His eyes met hers and held.

"I'm still scared to let myself get emotionally involved again. I don't know if I'll ever get past that. Rick says I shouldn't think about that. He says I should take each day and live it as fully as I can. He told me to keep repeating this verse from Psalms fiftieth chapter, verses fourteen and fifteen. It's God speaking. 'I want you to trust me in your times of trouble so I can rescue you and you can give me glory.'"

"That's a lesson we all need to learn and relearn," Alicia agreed, feeling a twinge of sadness that she wouldn't be the one he'd turn to. She glanced at the wall clock. "This has been wonderful, Jack, but perhaps we should get going. The boys will be waiting."

"Sure." He grinned at her. "Giselle made me promise we wouldn't get talking and end up coming late. She sure does love those stories of yours."

"Have you spoken to her about her birth mother yet?" she asked.

"A little. I warned her again that things might not turn out as she wanted, but that's all. I want to ease into it." He gave her an apologetic look. "She has such great expectations."

"They'll only get bigger," Alicia warned. She didn't say more because she knew he was struggling with himself over protecting his little girl. She rose when he held her chair, and preceded him out of the restaurant. "I can't thank you enough for that dinner. It was delicious."

"I can't thank you enough for helping with the

cleaning," he said. He threaded his arm around her waist, guiding her to his car.

Alicia paused, suddenly aware that she felt no inhibitions, no fear, no skittering sense of apprehension, as she had so often when a man had come too close. In fact, she wanted more. She wanted Jack to kiss her!

"Is something wrong?" he asked.

Alicia stared into his eyes and knew with soul-deep certainty that she had fallen in love with Jack Campbell. It should have made her happy.

Instead, all she could think about was how much he loved his daughter. Jack would never understand that she'd given her own child away and now had no clue where he was. And when he learned why, he'd despise her for it.

"Alicia?" He touched her chin so he could look into her eyes. "What's wrong?"

Everything.

"Just savoring the moment." The longings grew too strong. She lifted her hand and cupped his cheek in her palm. "Thanks for being my friend, Jack." She stood on tiptoe so she could once, just this one time, brush her lips against his cheek. "Thanks a lot."

Then she climbed into his car, her heart weeping as she repeated the Bible promise from Rick's last sermon.

I trust in the mercy of God forever and ever.

Chapter Twelve

"I'm sorry, Adam," Alicia said. "Hurtful words cut like no knife ever could."

"Maybe I deserve what the other kids said," Adam muttered. "After all, I was rude to you."

"I remember," Alicia murmured.

Jack froze at the corner of the sod house, conscious that the mid-August sun wasn't as warm as it had been. Alicia sat on a boulder in the sunshine with Adam, the smallest of the boys at Lives, their dark heads bent together as they talked. He doubted she even remembered he was there.

"As a kid I was called lots of horrible things. I didn't fit in, you see," she said softly. "I didn't have any friends and I was different than the others, so kids made fun of me."

Jack knew he was eavesdropping but couldn't tear himself away. Alicia had obviously suffered difficulties in her life. He needed to understand how those troubles had made her into the woman about whom everyone had something nice to say.

"You're small for your age, Adam, but so what?" Affection radiated through Alicia's words. "That's the way God made you."

"On purpose?" Adam asked.

"Of course." Alicia's laughter rang out. "You aren't an accident. You are a very precious child of the most high God. He loves every detail about you, that's why He made you this way." Her faith echoed in each word. "Your Father made you perfect. That's what you have to remember, not what others say."

Jack didn't hear any response so he peeked around the corner. Alicia was hugging the boy, her inner beauty shining through like a bright beam of sunshine.

"But they said I was a—" Adam spit out the ugly word and jerked away. Tears glittered on his cheeks. His jaw clenched. "I can't just forget that."

"Do you want to know what they called me?" One after another Alicia recited ugly racial slurs, her voice growing tighter with each one.

Jack's skin chilled at the viciousness. She'd been barely a teen, with no parents to encourage her. How had she remained so strong in her faith?

"Those words were like nails cutting into me." Her voice was raw. "Every day I'd come home, feeling like I was bleeding."

The agony in those words revealed her struggle to

regain control. Jack longed to go to her, to fold her in his arms and take away the pain, to replace those horrible words with the truth, that she was beautiful and very special. He wanted to, but he was desperately afraid to let go, to be vulnerable, to embrace what he felt—because he could lose it all again.

"So what did you do?" Adam's squeaky voice betrayed his inner tension.

"I suffered horribly until a friend reminded me that I had the armor of God. That if I put it on, those words couldn't hurt me. I'd imagine holding it in front of me so that those ugly words bounced off."

She stopped suddenly. Jack didn't understand why, he only knew that when she resumed speaking, her voice wobbled slightly.

"You have to stop letting them get to you, Adam." She brushed his cheek with her knuckles. "If you ever forget who you are again, come see me," she invited. "I'll remind you that God your Father doesn't make mistakes when He creates His kids."

It struck Jack then that Giselle's frequent questions about God might be something Alicia could help him answer. She obviously knew a lot about kids' fears. She'd reassured Adam so calmly, so matter-of-factly, that Adam now stood with confidence.

Hearing about Alicia's problems raised a new question. Was Giselle suffering with this move? If so, Alicia would know how to help his daughter.

He'd come to Alicia with a lot of problems. And

yet she'd never refused to help him. By contrast, it seemed he'd done very little for her. Maybe it was time to start.

"Hi, Jack. I'm glad you waited for me."

Jack startled. Alicia was standing at the corner. Her quizzical look lasted only a second before she quickly glanced away. That brief look raised questions. Alicia seemed more distant today. She didn't meet his gaze head-on, as usual.

"Actually, I wanted to give you some space with Adam," he told her. "What you said made me think about Giselle." Adam was busy smoothing the last bits of mud over the entry. He wouldn't overhear them. "Do you think Giselle might be having problems as a result of our move?"

"Why don't you ask her?" Alicia gave him a stern look. "You can't keep avoiding the tough subjects, Jack."

"I know, but I'm trying to let her come to me." He raked a hand through his hair. "She keeps asking me about God's will. I don't know how to answer."

"Honestly," Alicia advised.

The arrival of the boys cut off their discussion for the moment. Alicia put them all to work, including Garret, who was to take photos of the progress on the house. Then she returned to Jack.

"If Giselle has questions of faith, maybe she should talk to Pastor Rick," she suggested. "He's great with the boys from Lives."

Jack had been hoping Alicia would step in with
an answer, but now he had a sense she was putting
distance between them. He didn't blame her. He'd
already asked a lot of her. Giselle was in her store
constantly, seeking to understand Native culture, but
also, perhaps, because she found a kind of mother-
liness in Alicia. It had to be taxing on Alicia, who,
as a single woman, was used to being on her own,
doing her own thing.

Maybe she wanted to be free of him and Giselle
and their problems.

"I've been meeting with Rick a lot lately," he admitted.

Alicia gave him a quick sideways glance, but her
gaze didn't meet his.

Her eyes flared but Jack didn't want to get into it.
It was still too personal, so he said, "Shall we check
out our creation?"

"We should do a last inspection to make sure it's
all good. And then we should have a pizza party for
them." She nodded toward the boys, who were all
busy with the final touches on the house.

"Good idea." Jack walked around the structure
with Alicia at his side.

Pride swelled at what they'd created together. He
suppressed a laugh when she mentioned a new project she was considering. Alicia never stopped. Suddenly he wondered why he hadn't heard her speak

lately about opening a second store. She'd seemed very gung ho about it when he'd first arrived.

"Are you okay?" he asked when she checked over one shoulder, scanning the town as if she was looking for something.

"Of course." She flashed her lovely smile, although it didn't seem genuine to Jack.

That same uneasy feeling pricked his senses, but after a moment's consideration Jack brushed it away. This was Churchill. No criminals lurked around the corner here.

Their walk surveying the sod house proved one thing. It was ready for the celebration day tomorrow. Alicia called the group together.

"Everything looks great." Excitement threaded her words. This time she looked directly at him, her dark eyes sparkling. "I want to thank Jack for helping us with this project."

Jack waited for the applause to end.

"This was totally my pleasure." He gazed into Alicia's eyes, meaning every word. "I didn't think I wanted to do this at first. But look what we've built. It's amazing. Thank you, Alicia, for leading us."

Once again the boys whopped and hollered with their applause.

"The most important part of this sod house was you." Alicia exchanged a look with each boy. "Look what you did. You pushed through the rain and wind and ignored people who said it couldn't be done. You proved you could do it. You have helped make understanding Churchill's history easier. Was it worth it?"

Every single boy answered in a roar. "Yes!"

"Don't ever let anyone tell you that you can't do something. Put forward your best effort. Be proud of your work," she said. "I am."

Jack's chest swelled with pride for Alicia. She had a smear of mud on one cheek. Her hair had pulled free of its clasp and blew in the breeze. Her nails were smudged, her clothes filthy, and yet she glowed with a beauty that had nothing to do with her appearance.

Everything about Alicia Featherstone was lovely.

"I'm ready for pizza. Where's Giselle?" Alicia asked him.

"She'll be along. Let's go." Seeing Alicia's worry made Jack wish he hadn't promised to remain silent until Giselle unveiled her surprise.

Jack loved the lighthearted way Alicia bumped his shoulder as they walked toward the café. She teased the boys mercilessly so that everyone was laughing when they squeezed into the booths inside Polar Bear Pizzas. Obviously clued in ahead of time, owner Mindy Smart set pitchers of soda on each table. Alicia took note of each boy's favorite kind of pizza.

"What about Giselle? What kind does she like?" Because Alicia was squeezed beside him in the booth with the boys, her breath brushed his cheek as she shifted to get more comfortable.

"Giselle eats whatever kind of pizza there is. She's not picky." Jack didn't budge. Instead he swung his arm over the back of the seat so Alicia could slide nearer. He grinned when his daughter rushed through the door.

He wasn't as pleased when she scooted in beside Eli, but Alicia's talk with Adam had convicted Jack. He'd struggled to accept the boy's friendship with Giselle without knowing anything about him. A lot of people had done the same thing, prejudged Alicia. Seeing how deeply it had wounded her made Jack determined not to prejudge a kid.

He leaned back, content to let Alicia carry the conversation. She answered a thousand questions, announced the town crews would erect a sign at the sod house before the train arrived tomorrow morning and generally eased fears about whether their work was good enough.

"Come winter, we'll add a snow tunnel at the entrance," she promised. "That will keep the snow out of the house and cut down on the wind erosion."

There was a moment of silence as the boys realized that by winter they might have completed the sentence they'd been ordered to serve at Lives Under Construction, but Alicia quickly cheered them. When conversation left her free, Jack leaned closer.

"You have a knack with kids, Alicia. You should

have a bunch of your own." As soon as the words were out of his mouth he knew he'd said something wrong.

Her face paled. He thought she'd faint. Her hand shook as she reached out to take a drink. She avoided his gaze.

Jack didn't have a clue how to mend his mistake.

The pizza came and was devoured. Giselle made her announcement and showed off her handiwork. She held out a pair of leather slippers.

"Beading on moccasins like these was done during long cold winter nights and it was done by candlelight." She beamed with pride as Alicia admired her work. Then she continued with her next item. "Finger weaving was a fun way to create games and also decorate small bits of clothing. I'll show everyone how to do it tomorrow. This is a sash. Cree people made these to remember their ancestors just like we do with family trees."

"Amazing job, Giselle. These will all go in our house with Garret's photo book." She looked around at the faces at the table. "What a wonderful group to work with. As my thank-you, the cake's on me." Alicia's voice sounded normal, but Jack had a hunch she was hiding her emotions.

Alicia smiled as Mindy carried out a decorated cake with a little house outlined on it. After dessert, when Laurel arrived to take the boys home,

Alicia hugged each one, murmuring encouragement in every ear. She did the same to Giselle.

But when she turned to Jack he knew something was wrong. Her smile was too forced, her body too stiff.

"Thanks so much for all your help, too, Jack," she said, but she didn't look directly at him. "We've got a big day tomorrow. I suggest we relax tonight. Good night."

Jack watched her go, aching because something he'd said had obviously hurt her. He yearned to gather her in his arms and chase away whatever had her worried. But Alicia was an independent woman. She wouldn't cry on his shoulder. She was all about being strong and self-sufficient. She certainly wouldn't admit her problem to him.

"Is something bothering Alicia?" Giselle frowned as she watched her heroine walk away. "She seems sort of down."

"She's probably tired. So am I. Let's go home." He slung an arm around his daughter's shoulders. "About those questions you've been asking… I think we should see Pastor Rick together."

"Really, Dad?"

"Maybe he can help both of us." Jack noticed Giselle's focus was on Alicia, who stepped into her store.

"I wish we could do something for her," Giselle murmured, finally turning away to walk to the hotel with him. "I love Alicia. I want her to be happy." His daughter gazed up like a child who expected her parent to make everything okay. "Can't you do something, Daddy?"

"I wish I could, sweetheart." He brushed the bangs off her forehead and planted a kiss there. "But I don't know how to help Alicia." All he knew was that something about his comment that she should have kids had made her extremely sad.

In that moment Jack decided that if it took all night, he was going to figure out a way to make sure Alicia had a happy day tomorrow.

Six hours later, seated on his deck with his favorite latte in hand, Jack finally asked himself why Alicia's happiness mattered so much.

The answer scared the daylights out of him.

Because he wanted her in his life.

With all the risks that entailed.

"We haven't had so many summer tourists in town at one time for years," Lucy enthused. "I've already sold all of our hand-knit sweaters and socks and it's *hot* outside." Her gleeful tone died suddenly. She tipped her head to one side. "Are you coming down with something?"

"No. Just tired." Alicia knew Lucy had seen her staring out the window at Jack as he hurried past. "I've really appreciated you looking after the store for me while we worked on the sod house. I couldn't have done it otherwise."

"Sweetie, I'm delighted to have contributed. Hector will tell you that I'm useless when it comes to building things. Or climbing around on the rocks for that matter." She brushed the loose strands of hair off Alicia's face. "You did a wonderful thing. Now let me handle Tansi and you go enjoy that Inuit demonstration you nagged council to bring here."

"Thanks. I'll bring you some lunch," Alicia promised after pressing a kiss against Lucy's downy white curls.

"Oh, no thanks, dear. Hector's taken care of all that." She beamed as if a lunch with her husband of fifty-seven years was still a big deal.

"That's what I want," Alicia muttered as she strode toward the sod house. "An enduring love that doesn't diminish with age and time. Can You help me with that, Lord?"

The only response was the slap of her feet against the sidewalk. But the sight of the boys and Giselle gathered around the sod house and the new sign cheered her.

"Our house is open from one to five, so let's go enjoy the demonstration and then come back."

As they were leaving Jack, hurried over from the lodge to join them.

"I'm guessing you have a full house," Alicia said.

He grinned and Alicia caught her breath at his

handsome face. When she dared to dream of being married, it was Jack she saw in her future, laughing with her, enjoying the smallest events of life together: a picnic on the beach, a snowball fight, a Christmas Eve in front of the fire.

He'd tease, laugh at her in that cute way he had when the lines around his eyes fanned out and worry left his blue eyes. They'd have fun together. She'd show him the remote village where she'd lived with her parents, share how they'd influenced her life and talk about them as she'd seldom done. He'd show her his favorite haunts in Vancouver.

Maybe Jack would invite his friends here, introduce her to them. They would do all the silly things couples in love did: steal a kiss when no one was looking, hold hands under the table, write little love notes… Her heart stopped.

Even if these daydreams came true, even if he did write love notes, she couldn't read them. Lucy had tried to teach her but with little success. After some research she'd suggested that Alicia might have something called dyslexia. Alicia remembered that label from the Vancouver school where she'd been taking that special class with Mr. Parcet. She had made progress there, just not fast enough to keep up with the others in her class.

"Alicia?" Jack laid a hand on her arm. "We're here," he said, pointing to the tent perched on the bluff above the bay. "You haven't heard a word I said, have you?"

"Sorry," she apologized, and ducked her head to hide her burning cheeks. "I was thinking."

"You were worrying," he corrected. "About the house?" He shook his head in reproof. "Everything is perfect. Now relax and enjoy."

She drew a deep cleansing breath and nodded. "I'll try."

And in fact she did enjoy every moment. After an interesting presentation, extraordinary artifacts were unveiled and the history behind them explained. The caribou tent they'd erected was standing room only, so Alicia stood at the back beside Jack, enjoying the expression on his face as he heard of Native leaders' past customs.

When the presentation ended, the boys moved through the crowd, handing out pamphlets about the sod house which Jack, Garret and Giselle had photocopied. Then the mayor drew everyone's attention to the food booth set up in a central area where the Lives' boys would sell sandwiches and cold drinks to raise funds for a future project.

"That's our cue. Come on," Jack grabbed her hand and together they raced to the booth one of the service clubs had lent them. "Thank heaven for Hector," he said, watching as the older man hefted trays of sandwiches he'd brought from Lives.

"And Laurel. Without her, Lives Under Construc-

tion wouldn't exist and the boys wouldn't be here."
Alicia shared a smile with him and felt her heartbeat speed up. Jack grinned as he began to sell to
the assembling crowd. He was a perfect helpmate.

They worked side by side nonstop.

"I think we've finally fed almost everyone," she
said to Laurel more than an hour later. "Make sure
you tell Sara her brownies were the hottest seller."

"We all did well." Laurel shook her head as she
looked at Alicia. "You look like you could use a
break. Jack left to make sure all's well at the sod
house, but I saved a sandwich for you. Better take
off that apron. You have soda all over it."

"One of the Brown kids shook their root beer. I'm
wearing most of it." Alicia undid the sticky apron.

Just before she tucked it away, she remembered
the note Giselle had given her from Jack. She
reached into the apron pocket, but the napkin was
soaked with soda and the ink had run so that even
if she could read, the words were impossible to decipher.

She tucked it into her jeans pocket anyway. A
note from Jack was to be treasured no matter what
it said. The idea of soda did not appeal, so Alicia
walked over to Common Grounds and ordered a
cup of coffee to go.

"The presentation was a big success," Mindy said
as she handed over the cup. "Good for you for thinking of it. Someday, when you have time, I'd love you

to bring something over for our display cases." She tilted her head. "I think telling our history to tourists is a great idea."

"I'll think of something," Alicia promised with a smile. She left the café deep in thought about Mindy's offer and dearly wishing Jack was there so she could tell him about it. Sharing with Jack had become her priority and now everything she did was couched in, *What would Jack think?*

She was beginning to want his opinion on everything!

"Come with me. Make a sound and you'll wish you hadn't." Strong fingers closed around her arm, almost dragging her toward the church.

Her head jerked toward the voice. *No!*

"Wh-what are you doing here, Mr. Parcet?" Alicia rasped, every nerve in her body seething with loathing. "What do you want?"

"As if you didn't know." He dragged her behind the church.

People were looking at her oddly, so Alicia went along, knowing that if she yelled or asked for help there would be too many questions. And she did *not* want to explain.

"Where's your kid?" Jeremy Parcet shoved her against the stone side of the church and put his hands on either side of her head so that she had to look at him. "Tell me where he is or I'll tell these new friends of yours all about your past, how you gave yourself to any man with money when you walked the streets in Vancouver."

"That isn't true!"

"Think anyone will believe that?" he sneered.

"I'll tell them what you did," she said in an almost-whisper because her shame was so great.

"Like I said before, who will believe you? You'd have to produce the kid." He stood back, his face dark with foreboding. "I don't want him, if that's what you're worried about. Not a half-breed."

The ugly word sickened her. But Mr. Parcet was not finished. He leaned in close, his face so near she could feel his breath on her face. Her stomach threatened to turn.

"I just want a blood test so I can collect my inheritance. Then your brat can go back to whatever slum he's living in." His fingers were now like handcuffs on her wrist. "I'll give you two weeks. If you don't tell me where he is, everyone in this sad little town is going to hear all about the secret life of Alicia Featherstone. Who do you think they'll believe?"

Feeling physically ill, Alicia pressed against the wall as hard as she could and prayed for help. Suddenly Rick's voice resounded from the window above their heads, the open window of his office. Clearly startled, Mr. Parcet loosened his grip. Alicia seized her opportunity and broke free. She raced around the side of the church and hurried inside the cool, dim sanctuary.

There she huddled, heart hammering, until she heard the train whistle. Mr. Parcet would be on it when it left in a few hours, she knew that. No way would he stay in Churchill, the *sad little* town. Only it wasn't. Churchill was Alicia's home and she loved it.

How could God have let Mr. Parcet come here? How could He have let this man hurt her again?

And all she could think was, if Jack knew, if he heard Mr. Parcet's story, he would despise her. Alicia didn't think she could stand to see that in his eyes.

After all her preaching about faith, God had let her down.

Now there was nowhere to turn.

Chapter Thirteen

Jack paced across the beach, ignoring the jagged-edged stones that hurt his feet. He could hardly wait for Alicia to meet him here for lunch. He'd been reasonably confident it was the right thing to do. After all, he'd spent a lot of time praying about it last night as Rick had suggested. When dawn arrived, it seemed to Jack that God was leading him to Alicia.

The idea of letting someone get close again scared him to death. But Rick had urged him to stop living in fear and explore his growing feelings for Alicia, and Jack had decided last night that Alicia was worth the risk. That's why he'd put together this picnic and lugged the basket down here.

He'd sent the note with Giselle to be certain Alicia wouldn't miss or misplace it again. But she still wasn't here. Maybe someone had stopped her at the sod house. Jack climbed back up the beach and surveyed the town site. But Alicia wasn't at the sod house.

Then he saw someone in a red shirt emerge from Common Grounds. Certain it was Alicia, he started walking toward her, intending to call out. Suddenly a man grabbed her arm, said something to her, and Alicia walked with him toward the church.

The man looked familiar and Jack searched his mind, his mouth pursing as he watched the man put his arms on either side of Alicia's head, preventing her from leaving. In that moment Jack remembered the guy—a teacher, the bad-boy son of a wealthy father. He also remembered the case the man had been involved in. A coworker had made allegations about this guy. He hadn't been cleared per se, but Daddy's hotshot lawyer had pulled strings so the charges had been dropped. The complainant had suddenly refused to talk and Jack had been forced to close the case. He remembered that the woman had moved away.

How did Alicia know scum like Jeremy Parcet?

His phone rang. It was Giselle.

"Daddy? I'm at Alicia's store and I can't reach her. Lucy isn't feeling well. Can you get Hector to come and take her home? I'll stay here."

Jack agreed and hung up. He could no longer see Alicia, but Parcet was heading toward the train station. It wouldn't leave for another three hours but, knowing Parcet, Jack figured he'd sit inside the old station rather than explore the sights of Churchill.

"Good," he muttered. "Leave here and stay gone. Leave Alicia alone."

His temper simmered as he thought of Alicia around a guy like that. He took a quick scan of the area again, but she'd disappeared. With a sigh for the basket of lunch he'd left on the beach, Jack jogged over to the sod house, gave Hector the information and complimented the boys on the great job they were doing.

"A man asked me to send him some of my pictures," Garret told him, holding out a card. "He really liked my work."

"Of course he did, because it's amazing." Jack congratulated him. "Have you seen Alicia?"

"She was talking to some creepy guy," Rod told him.

"She ran into the church," Matt said. "She looked upset."

"Thanks, guys. Keep up the good work."

The kids didn't need him. They were busy showing every detail to people who'd lined up for a look inside the sod house. He headed for the church. It was dim inside and quiet, so quiet he could hear faint sniffs and a scared voice whispering, "Please, God…"

His radar went off. Something was very wrong.

"Alicia?" He walked slowly down the aisle until he finally saw her hunkered down in a pew.

Her face was as pale as he'd ever seen it. One

of her braids had come undone and her hair was a mess. Her shirt was torn, her face was covered in tears and she was visibly shaking.

Burning inside because he knew Parcet had done this, Jack sat down and drew her into his arms. She grabbed hold of him as if he was a lifeline in very rough seas. Jack reveled in the sweet delight of holding her, but he suppressed that to concentrate on soothing her, until he realized that she was desperately troubled.

"You're okay, sweetheart," he crooned. "You're safe. You're here with me and nobody's going to hurt you. He didn't hurt you, did he?" he asked as worry surged.

"Wh-who?"

"Jeremy Parcet. I saw him talking to you."

She went very still in his arms. Her brown eyes grew huge. "You *know* him?" she whispered.

"Oh, I know him all right. I've investigated him a couple of times, though I never got to arrest him, more's the pity." He frowned. "How do you know him?"

"A long time ago he was m-my teacher," she whispered. Then the tears welled again, pouring down her face. "Don't ask me any more about it. Please, Jack? I don't want to remember him—those days. There's too much unhappiness."

Jack smoothed her cheek, removing the damp tears.

"But what does someone like you have to do with someone like him?" he asked. "He's not your kind."

"My *kind*?" Her big brown eyes gaped. "What do you mean?"

"You're good and decent and caring. You give to people, you don't take like he does." Jack paused, searching for words to express how much she was coming to mean to him. "You're pure and shining and he's dirty and dingy." Jack stopped because Alicia pressed her cheek against his chest and wrapped her arms even more tightly around him.

"You don't really know me," she sobbed. "I'm not like that."

"To me you are." His lips grazed her neck. Jack loved the feeling of her silky skin, loved the way she turned to him, the way she fit in his embrace as if she belonged there. "That's what I wanted to tell you at our picnic." He couldn't rid himself of the image of Parcet holding her. "But you didn't come. Was it because of him? I don't understand—"

"I can't explain," she whispered, her face glistening with fresh tears. "Can't you trust me, Jack? Please?" Her eyes begged him and he could not deny her.

"Of course I trust you, Alicia." He tightened his hold. "You're safe with me. Someday I hope you'll explain. But just know that while I'm here he can't get to you."

"Thank you." She rested her head on his shoulder. All the fight went out of her as she exhaled. It was as if she had no more energy, as if all she could do was breathe.

Jack smoothed a hand up and down her back, whispering words of comfort he hoped would take away the terror he sensed was still crouched inside her mind. He wouldn't press her for an answer now. But later…later he'd find out why Jeremy Parcet terrified Alicia.

They sat together a long time, quietly. Gradually Alicia's breathing evened. Jack had no sense of time. He only knew his arms weren't ready to let her go when she drew back.

"Thank you, Jack."

He couldn't stop himself from leaning forward and pressing his lips to hers. It was what he'd wanted to do for weeks now and once his lips met hers, he knew it was right. For a second Alicia froze. He drew back, cupped her lovely face in his hands.

"It's okay," he whispered. "I will never hurt you."

"I know. You're not that kind of man. That's what I lo—like about you." After a fraction of a second she leaned forward to kiss him.

As the kiss deepened, asking, answering, Jack knew she'd been going to say *love*. He'd seen it in her eyes, known it from the way her lips answered his. She loved him. Since that was exactly how he felt about her, Jack tried to show it in his kiss. He had a feeling he'd succeeded when she drew away, breathless.

"The boys will be wondering where we are. We should join them." Alicia kept her eyes down, her gaze hidden. Shy, sweet Alicia.

"I think you should change your shirt first. It's torn here on the sleeve." Jack loved that she was innocent enough to blush when he tipped her chin up to look into her eyes. He smoothed a finger over the rip, forcing down the rage that swelled inside at the thought of Parcet doing this.

Alicia went white when she stared at the tear.

"I'll wait till you return, then walk back with you."

She nodded before hurrying away.

Jack sat in the coolness of the church, trying to understand the emotions surging within him. He loved Alicia. In fact, he'd loved her for a while. He just hadn't wanted to admit it because the thought of losing her scared him to death.

"You look frustrated."

At the sound of the voice, Jack turned to see Rick sit down beside him.

"Can I help?" the pastor asked.

"I just figured out I love Alicia," Jack said, unwilling to pretend when he so desperately needed help. "I'd almost decided this afternoon that God had led me to her. Then this. What do I do now?" he asked the pastor.

"Why do you have to do anything?" Rick leaned back in the pew. "Why can't you just relax, enjoy your relationship with Alicia and see where God leads?"

"Because I want to prepare myself." Jack blinked at the bare truth of it.

"Prepare yourself for what?" Rick studied him with a frown.

"In case something happens," he said, feeling his way through.

"Will that make it easier? Will it be okay to love her then? Tell me how you make loving someone and then losing them okay."

It sounded ridiculous when Rick said it that way.

"Life is a journey, my friend. There are detours and accidents all over. You do the best you can, but you can't always be prepared. Sometimes you have to lean on God to get you through." Rick rose at the sound of the church door opening. "It's all about trust, Jack. You've got to let go of the controls and trust God." He stepped into the aisle. "Hey, Alicia. Congrats. The sod house is a marvel."

"Thanks. We're proud of the boys and Giselle." She looked at Jack. "Lucy's out sick and nothing I can say will persuade Giselle that she isn't in charge. She ordered me out of my own store."

She looked so shocked Jack smothered his amusement.

"Well, she is her father's daughter," Rick teased.

"I'm late for a canoe ride with Kyle and you know he'll make me paddle him for miles. See you."

Jack rose as Rick left. He walked beside Alicia to the sod house, where the boys were jubilant with the visitors' comments. They closed up the house, handed Alicia the key and left with Laurel and Teddy, who'd offered to barbecue burgers for dinner.

"I'm starved, too," Alicia said.

"My picnic!" Jack took her hand and urged her toward the beach. "It's still here. Amazing. Come and sit down." He began building a small fire out of driftwood because a beach picnic seemed to demand a fire. "Did you get my note this time?"

Alicia pulled the damp napkin from her pocket with a wry grin. "I got it, but—"

"We need a different means of communication," he told her. The fire threatened to go out so he blew on it.

"I may be pure Indian but I don't do smoke signals, Jack," she said, coughing as the smoke blew in her face.

Jack chuckled as he handed her a sandwich. He held her hand when she would have drawn away.

"I like being with you, Alicia."

"I like being with you, too," she whispered, meeting his gaze for a moment before her lashes fell. That was enough for now, Jack thought, remembering Rick's advice.

"This is very good," she complimented as she ate.

She sat back on the blanket and he could practically feel peace settle on her like dew on grass.

Jack hated to bring up the subject but now seemed the perfect time, and he needed to understand.

"Can you tell me what happened between you and Parcet, Alicia?" he asked. "I know something's wrong. Please let me help."

At the mention of his name the tension began humming around her. "There's nothing you can do," she said, waving her hand as if to shoo away the topic. "But thank you."

He had to let it go. As they continued to eat, they chatted about the Celebration Day events. Then suddenly Alicia sat up straight.

"Oh, I forgot. Giselle asked me if I knew what you learned from that letter that came from the adoption agency yesterday. She's very curious, but she doesn't want to bug you. Can you tell me what it said? Do they have news about her birth mom yet?"

"I doubt it." He grimaced. "The letter was just another form I haven't yet filled out. I—uh, haven't done much about pursuing that line lately."

"Oh, Jack, why? Giselle is the most important person in your life. Don't you love her enough to find the truth?"

The question stunned him.

"Of course I love her. I want what's best for her." He was miffed that she'd brought up the subject again. "But how could it be better for her to know her past than to be safe with me?"

"It's not a matter of better." Alicia's hand curled around his. She waited until he was looking at her before she spoke again. "It's because she needs all the pieces of the past to put together who she is. She's desperate to know the truth, Jack. She even asked me to talk to you, ask you to keep pressing for information."

"I don't want to," he admitted on a slow exhale.

"I know." Sympathy filled her voice, but underlying that lay a steely determination. "I wonder why that is. Could it be because you're afraid Giselle will want a relationship with her birth parents and you'll be left alone?"

"You think I'm feeling left out?" He jumped to his feet to vent his frustration. "I'm trying to keep her safe."

"But not knowing is making her insecure." Alicia rose, placed her hand on his arm. "Giselle will always love you. You're her dad. No one can take your place. But the heart can grow. It can accommodate lots of love. Don't you want that for your child?"

Jack had no answer. They finished their picnic in a much more somber mood and more quickly than he'd intended. He walked Alicia home, read the note on the door and shook his head.

"Giselle says she's gone out to Lives with Rick.

We're supposed to join them for a campfire." He looked at her. "Want to?"

"Of course. We must celebrate their success." Alicia walked to the truck with him and climbed in.

Jack was filled with foreboding. What if Alicia was right? What if he refused to find her birth mom and Giselle went looking on her own? All kinds of things could happen, and he wouldn't be in control of them.

Maybe it was time to finish the investigation, to get *all* the facts and then figure out how to tell his daughter. The only good part was that he knew he could count on Alicia to deal with the outcome. She was one amazing woman. God *was* drawing them together.

It would just take time.

Jack helped Alicia into the truck. "Nice celebration, huh?"

"Very nice." To hide her reaction to his touch, she made small talk about the evening's campfire— they'd roasted marshmallows and played games— and she described the boys' quest for a new project. She even brought up the intriguing possibility of a relationship between Laurel and Teddy Stonechild, but Jack barely answered.

Silence fell.

Obviously Jack didn't want to talk during the ride home from Lives, but Alicia needed this time alone with him to make him understand Giselle's point of view. Luckily the girl had taken up Rick's offer of an ATV ride to take her home.

"You've been very kind to me, Jack. I treasure that. I've never known a man like you. You're honest and decent and you care about people." Alicia mentally pushed away all those wonderful memories of being in his arms. She couldn't dream about that now. She'd save them for later, when she was alone. "I know you're trying to protect Giselle."

"Always," he said.

"But don't you see," she coaxed. "You're not protecting her. You're trying to wrap her in cotton wool instead of preparing her to deal with whatever life hands her. I know because it's the same thing my parents did."

He frowned, looking at her sideways. "What do you mean?"

"We lived in a little isolated village. Everyone was like me. I didn't know I was different." She closed her eyes at the memories. "We seldom went to town—it was too far. But if we did, my parents sheltered me from everything. I didn't know bias and racism existed until I moved to Vancouver. Then I didn't know how to deal with it."

Jack peered ahead, his face tight.

"If they'd only prepared me, I doubt I'd have gotten into trouble."

"What trouble?" he asked.

"Lots." She worried her lips, hating this part but knowing it had to be said. "I did some things as a teen that I didn't know how to get out of it."

"Most teens do." He brushed it off.

"Maybe. But I don't want Giselle to end up like I did."

"Why would she?" he asked. "I'll be here."

"But you can't prevent everything. Someday she'll be on her own, all alone. Don't you want her to be able to figure out how to deal with issues rather than flounder and fear?" By the set of his jaw, Alicia knew he wasn't hearing her. "I care for you, Jack. That's why I'm going to say this. You're a wonderful dad, but you're trying to control Giselle instead of doing what a loving father should."

"And what's that?" he muttered.

"Preparing your kid for her future. That's a parent's real job, to teach independence." She hated hurting him but she forced herself to continue. "Give Giselle the truth and let her judge for herself. If she makes a mistake, you be there, help her get up and face the next challenge. That's what real fatherhood is all about."

Her heart swelled with love for this decent, caring man. He was so protective of Giselle because he loved her. The world could be a nasty place; Jack had certainly seen a lot of that in his line of work. How could he not be afraid for his daughter? But his fear couldn't override the need for his daughter to feel empowered, and how could she do that if she didn't get her questions answered?

"How do you know so much about parenthood, Alicia?" Jack asked as he stopped the truck in front of her store.

She smiled because she knew there was no malice in his question. He was hurting. He wanted a way out and there was none.

Jack was a man among men. In him she'd finally found the love she'd always craved. But Jack couldn't love her. Not really. He wanted perfect, like Simone, and Alicia was damaged. Though he might feel sorry for her, Jack would never be able to see past her mistakes or understand why she'd made them.

He came around to open her door and she climbed out of the truck. She stepped directly in front of him, her face inches from his.

"I know that the hardest part of parenting is letting go of your kid." She fought back the emotions in order to finish. "Sooner or later you are going to have to let Giselle go, Jack. Will she be ready to take on life?"

His face altered as pain and angst and a hundred other emotions crowded in. He was so dear, so precious, the most wonderful man in the world. Casting aside all inhibition, Alicia stepped forward and wrapped her arms around his waist. She brushed her lips against the corner of his mouth then slid them up his jaw to the tip of his ear.

"You're a good man, Jack Campbell. Thank you for being my friend."

She kissed him once more, a kind of farewell kiss directly on the lips. Then she hurried away, anxious to be alone with memories of the only love she'd ever known. But even after she'd savored them, from the glory of his strong powerful arms around her to the brush of his bristly chin against her skin, to the strong minty flavor of his breath; even as she tucked away the feelings of security he'd given after Mr. Parcet had terrified her, Alicia knew one thing.

Even though Jack would never understand, even though he would see her as undeserving and uncaring if he knew the truth, if she had it to do again, she'd still give away her child to be loved by someone else.

"I feel alone and scared, God," she whispered, staring at the darkening sky. "There's no one who would understand why I had to do what I did but You. Take care of Jack and Giselle. And help me find a way to keep Mr. Parcet away."

Chapter Fourteen

"Good news, Jack."

Two weeks later his lawyer sounded jubilant on the phone. Jack wished he shared the enthusiasm, but some niggle of worry kept his alert level on high.

"The court has answered the special petition you had me file asking them to open Giselle's adoption records," the lawyer continued. "The judge felt that since her mother is dead there's no reason to keep the file sealed. I received the information and had it couriered to you. It should be delivered today."

"I just received it. Thanks." Jack hung up, dazed, slightly off-kilter as he stared at the manila envelope on the table.

So they were finally going to know the truth. Somehow it seemed anticlimactic. All this time he'd feared knowing and now the truth lay in front of him, fresh from the newly arrived train. All he had to do was tear it open. Then he'd know everything.

His old nemesis fear sent a shiver through him. He'd read it first, before—

"Jack?" Alicia stood on the deck, staring at him. "What's wrong?"

"Nothing. Everything." He held up the envelope. "Giselle's birth history."

Alicia sat down, watching him but saying nothing.

"I filed a special petition to open her case and the judge agreed."

"I'm so proud of you for doing that," she said. "I know how hard it was for you, but I also know how much Giselle wants to know her roots. Are you relieved?" she asked when he didn't immediately respond.

"*Surprised* is a better word. It's happened too fast." He soaked in the beauty of her face, acknowledging, if only to himself that he'd missed her these past two weeks. She'd gone on another of her stock trips and he'd been on tenterhooks waiting for her return. Thank heaven, Giselle was back at school and didn't question him too much.

"You look good," he said quietly. It wasn't the truth. Alicia looked thin and pale and very worried. The joy had disappeared from her eyes.

"No, I don't," she said with a mocking smile. "But thanks for pretending."

"Parcet bothering you again?" Jack didn't miss the tiny shudder she gave at the name. "I can—"

"No, I haven't seen him." She glanced at him then

quickly looked away. "I came to show you something." She pulled a clipping out of her pocket. "Lucy cut it out of the Winnipeg paper while I was away. She says we both got very good coverage."

She handed it to him, her hand skittering away when it brushed his. Jack studied her as he took it, but Alicia didn't look at him. She seemed fixated on something else, something that was troubling her. He had to find out what that was.

"It talks about Tansi and your hotel and us," she told him. "It even talks about the need for a store like mine in Winnipeg."

Jack scanned the article and thought how he hated the notion of her leaving. Not seeing her every day was unacceptable.

"That's your dream," he said, smiling into her lovely eyes. "Now you can go ahead. Can't you?"

"Maybe." She didn't sound thrilled. She just kept looking at him, staring actually, as if they'd been apart for too long. And they had. Jack had missed her so much.

"Alicia, I want to thank you—"

"Alicia! You're back." Giselle bounded up the stairs and swooped down to envelop Alicia in a hug. "Boy, we missed you. Dad's been like an old grump without you here to cheer him up."

"I doubt that's the reason," Alicia demurred. Not for the first time Jack wondered what had caused her lack of self-confidence. "You look happy. What's up?"

"Eli and I have decided on a new project," Giselle announced. "We're hoping you and Dad will help us," she said, a twinkle in her eyes. "You work so well together."

Alicia glanced at Jack. He rolled his eyes and groaned.

"What's the project?" Alicia asked.

"A tourist center. This town needs one." Giselle babbled on about the idea.

Jack nodded and murmured approval once in a while, but his attention was fixated on the envelope. He finally slid it toward himself and opened it, perusing the contents. His stomach clenched. His body went icy-cold despite the sun's warmth.

He carefully folded the documents and stuffed them back inside.

"What's that?" Giselle poked at the envelope.

"As I was telling Alicia, I just received your birth history, Giselle."

Jack noted the way Alicia touched her shoulder, offering comfort and support.

Alicia had become like a mom for his daughter, supportive, nurturing. Jack hoped she'd support him now, because he needed time to ease into this.

"Really, Daddy?" Giselle's dark eyes glowed with excitement.

"Remember I told you your birth mom had died?" he said carefully.

Giselle nodded. "You mean I'll finally know why she gave me up?" She grinned, narrowing her gaze. "Maybe my birth father died and she couldn't go on without him so she died of a broken heart. Or maybe…" The romantic dreams continued but Jack could hardly bear to listen.

"Aren't you going to tell her what's in there?" Alicia asked in a very soft voice, leaning close so Giselle wouldn't overhear.

Reluctantly he removed the papers.

"Maybe you should read them first, Alicia. You'd be able to soften things for her." Jack held the neatly typed report toward Alicia. "You'll be able to find the right words," he said, trying to express his plea for help.

"I don't think it's any of my business, Jack." Alicia backed away. "I think I should leave."

Jack rose, went to her.

"Please help me," he whispered for her ears alone. "Please. I don't think I can do this on my own. If you read the first page you'll understand why."

He didn't understand the odd look on her face, or the way she glanced at the papers as if she hadn't a clue what they said. He didn't know why she closed her eyes or chose that moment to whisper a prayer. All he knew was that it was right to have Alicia here. She belonged with them.

"What's wrong?" Giselle demanded, finally emerging from her happily-ever-after dream.

"Your dad asked me to read this," Alicia said. Then to Jack's horror she held the folded papers out to Giselle. "But that's not right. It's your life, your history. You should read what it says."

"No," he yelled, but Alicia shook her head.

"Her mother made a very hard choice when she gave up Giselle," Alicia whispered. Her cheeks paled. "I think Giselle deserves the right to know why."

Giselle studied the documents. Jack wanted to rip them from her hands and burn them. Why had he given them to Alicia? Hadn't she read anything? How could she be so cavalier?

He heard Giselle gasp and knew the worst was about to happen.

"My mother got pregnant with me after—" Giselle gasped, hesitated. "She was attacked by a family friend," she whispered.

Alicia's audible gasp showed her shock and proved she hadn't read a word. Why? He'd thought her the most caring woman in the world. What a mistake.

"She t-told her parents," Giselle continued, her confidence visibly shaken. "But they denied it, called her a liar and sent her away. They said she couldn't come home unless she had an…abortion. Oh, Daddy." Huge tears flooded Giselle's face as she gazed at him.

Jack thought his heart would rip out of his body at her pain.

"I was a mistake. My own grandparents wanted to—" She couldn't repeat the ugly word. She stared at the papers as if they were venomous snakes. "Alicia?"

But though Alicia's mouth opened, she couldn't speak. She stared at him. "I'm sorry," she finally whispered. "I'm so sorry."

"What good is that?" Jack demanded, furious with her. He flung an arm around Giselle's shoulder and hugged her close. "Read it all," he told her gently. "Then we'll put it away and forget it."

"Forget it?" She shook her head as she read further. "Daddy, how am I supposed to forget that I'm the product of an attack? How do I forget that she agreed to my adoption on the condition that you and Mom never search for her as long as she lived? How do I forget she died when I was two, on the streets?" she wailed. "I'm a mistake!"

"No you're not, sweetheart. You were never a mistake. You were the best thing that ever happened to us."

But Giselle wouldn't listen, wouldn't be consoled. "Honey, I know you dreamed it would be different, but—"

"Leave me alone!" Giselle threw the papers on the floor, then raced out of the room.

The silence in the room cut so deep, it hurt. Jack turned on Alicia.

He'd lost his daughter and it was her fault.

Alicia's heart ached for Jack's loss. Another part cringed, knowing she deserved his anger. Why couldn't she read?

"Giselle needs time to deal with this, Jack," she whispered. "It's better for her to know the truth than to try to keep it from her."

"Is it?" His lips curled.

"God will heal her pain. She just needs time." It sounded weak even in her own ears. And it did nothing to alleviate the pain she saw roiling in his eyes. Her heart ached to erase it but she'd lost that chance. Because she'd been so sure she had the answers.

"Did you even bother to read one sentence?" he asked, his voice forlorn.

"No." This was the time for honesty. Alicia shook her head.

"Why not? Why did you think I asked you to read it? The first line should have alerted you to the potential damage this could do." He picked the paper off the floor and shook it at her.

"I didn't read it, Jack," Alicia whispered. "Because I *can't* read."

"What?" He looked at her in disbelief. "You run a business…"

"Which Lucy helps with. She and some friends

helped me fill out the loan papers, do the books, all the things I can't do." Alicia took pity on his confusion. She'd hurt him too much. Better to be up front and face the disgust she knew she'd see in his face when he knew the truth. "I'm good at faking it, Jack. It was easy in my village. Later, when I was sent to Vancouver it got much harder but I faked my way through, used my government allowance to pay people to do my homework, let them put me in a slower track. I did whatever I had to in order to survive."

She saw the loathing creep in like a storm cloud, darkening his face. That's when she knew that he could never love her. Men like him, strong, independent men who were on top of their game, didn't fall for women who were easily conned by men like Jeremy Parcet. He'd be ashamed of her, embarrassed for her to know his friends. Not that she'd ever meet them. Jack was a proud man. He wouldn't want a girlfriend who couldn't even read.

How had she ever imagined he could care for her?

"It doesn't make sense." He was clearly thinking back. "The library—you ordered those books."

"I gave them your list," she reminded him, glancing at her watch.

"You can tell time."

"I learned to tell time and very basic arithmetic from my friends. They own a learning center in Vancouver. Nancy and Harold helped me get off the street, got me some good people to teach me the basics to live on my own. Lately Lucy's been trying to teach me to read but I'm lousy at it." She scrounged up a smile. "She thinks I'm dyslexic. That's why I can't read."

Alicia knew then that she could never tell him about her baby. He'd despise her even more; probably think the worst of her, as Mr. Parcet had said. Maybe he'd even believe she deserved what had happened. She couldn't take that. Some secrets had to be kept. For now.

"I'm so sorry I hurt Giselle," she whispered. "I care about her. And you. I only wanted the two of you to be happy."

Jack's lips tightened but he said nothing.

"I think I know where she's gone. I'll find her and bring her home. Don't worry, Jack." With one last look of longing at him, Alicia left.

She set off toward the sod house, knowing that was where Giselle would run. The young girl loved romantic images of the past. Alicia envied her. How she wished she could recapture her own innocence. But that was gone. Now she was alone.

Worse, she still hadn't found her son. Had Mr. Parcet?

But worst of all, Jack loathed her, was embarrassed by her. He'd never want anything to do with her again. Once more the memories of those few minutes he'd comforted her in the church filled her senses. He'd been so caring, so gentle. So loving.

Must I give Jack up, too, Lord?

Yes. The only thing this wonderful man wanted was his daughter. She would help Jack regain his most precious possession.

And then Alicia would be alone with only a memory of love.

Chapter Fifteen

Jack followed Alicia at a distance. When she went inside the sod house, he moved to the side and stood beside the small window, feeling guilty about listening in but determined to check on his baby girl.

"Are you okay, Giselle?" Alicia asked quietly.

"I don't think I'll ever be okay," his daughter answered in a muffled tone. "It's horrible, ugly. It's not the story I wanted."

"Why not? It's clear your mother loved you very much." Alicia spoke in a calm, soothing voice.

"How do you know?" Was that hope in his daughter's voice?

"She must have, because she didn't have an abortion. Instead she ran away, gave up her whole family just so she could have you. Then she gave you up because she wanted you to have a full, rich life. That sounds like a mother who loved you very much." Alicia paused.

"I don't know. It's just so sad."

"It is, isn't it? But sometimes God uses sad things."

Jack wondered if he should go inside. He decided to wait and let Alicia talk.

After a moment she said, "Can I tell you a story?"

"I guess." Giselle sniffed.

"I knew a girl once. She tried very hard to be a good girl but some bad things happened to her, and, like your mom, she got pregnant when she was very young. It wasn't her fault. She was attacked. Anyway, she had her baby, a little boy. He was so precious, with amazing fingers and toes. He made these little cooing sounds when she touched his face." Alicia stopped, her voice brimming with emotion. "He was the most precious thing she'd ever seen and she loved him with all her heart."

Jack frowned. The story sounded so...personal.

"But this girl knew she wasn't good enough to keep her baby and be his mother. She didn't know anything about being a mother. Besides, she couldn't give him a nice home, or toys or enough food to eat. In fact, she had nothing to give this baby. Nothing but love."

"So what did she do?" Giselle asked.

"She signed papers so he could be adopted by people who would love and take care of him, who would teach him how to be a child of God. And then she never saw him again. She wished many times that she could know he was all right, that he was loved, that he would know she never regretted having him. But she gave him away."

Jack could hear the tears in Alicia's voice and they wrenched at his heart so badly he longed to hold her in his arms and soothe them away. Who was she talking about?

"Do you think she was a good mom, Giselle?" Alicia asked.

"I think she was the best mom that boy could have. She put him first." Giselle sniffed. "It was you, wasn't it, Alicia? You were the baby's mom."

"Yes. I loved him so much."

Stunned by what he'd heard, Jack remained frozen in place. Alicia was a mother. She'd had a child she'd given up.

And yet, Alicia Featherstone was love. She lived it. She breathed it.

After a while Jack realized that no one was talking. He peeked in the window. Alicia, eyes closed, was holding Giselle in her arms. She would have been a perfect mother. She didn't sidestep hard issues. Instead, she confronted them and worked through the problem.

No one could pity Alicia Featherstone. Nothing had stopped her from rebuilding her life, from giving back to her community and every tourist who came through her store. He knew more clearly than he ever had that Giselle was safe in her hands.

Quietly Jack crept away. He found himself heading to the church, where he spent a long time asking God for help.

Alicia had been right. No matter how he phrased it, he could not have protected Giselle from her past. But he could be there for her whenever she needed his help.

Dare Jack trust God enough to trust Him with his heart?

Alicia was walking Giselle out of the sod house when a shadow darkened the doorway. Expecting Jack, she looked up. Instead Mr. Parcet loomed there.

Fear turned her blood cold.

"Your time is up, Alicia," he snarled as he grabbed her arm. "Now I'm going to tell the town all about you, unless you tell me where the kid is."

"You'll never know," she spat out. He jerked her forward, holding her wrists.

At that moment Giselle jumped toward him and yelled, "Let her go." She tugged at him.

Mr. Parcet slapped her away, knocking her off balance. Giselle stumbled on the uneven floor and toppled over, hitting her head on the corner of the homemade washstand she'd insisted on including.

"Giselle!" Alicia screamed. She broke free and rushed to kneel beside this child she'd gladly give her life for. "Wake up, sweetie." She kept repeating it until Giselle blinked and looked at her through bleary eyes. "Are you okay?"

"Leave the brat. You're coming with me." Mr. Parcet grabbed her arm, but Alicia was no longer afraid of him. She'd lost Jack. Giselle had been hurt. There was nothing else to save. She broke his grip, looked him straight in the eye as her heart prayed for help.

"I'll go with you," she said quietly. "Just let me call her dad." Without breaking her stare she hit speed dial and as soon as she heard Jack pick up, she said, "You do know who Giselle is, don't you, Mr. Parcet?"

"What do I care who she is?" he snarled. "Come on, we're leaving." He dragged her to her feet and pulled her toward the door.

"Sure." Alicia pretended nonchalance. "But I think you do know her dad. Jack Campbell. That's Detective Jack Campbell from Vancouver." She watched his face whiten. "I take it you remember him."

"Why you—" Mr. Parcet hadn't dragged her three steps when an ice-cold snarl sounded from outside.

"I'd advise you to let go of my fiancée and step back, Jeremy."

"Your—" Mr. Parcet gave a hoot of derisive laughter. "You're engaged to *her?*" A string of horrible words streamed from his mouth.

"Shut up." Jack stepped forward, his fist clenched.

"He hurt Giselle," Alicia said, shamed by Parcet's

awful words but desperate to insure Giselle was okay. Besides, she was afraid for Jack. She didn't want him hurt because of her.

She didn't know where the fiancée thing came from. It gave her goose bumps to imagine being engaged to Jack, but she'd daydream about that impossibility later.

"Giselle? Hurt—" Jack didn't finish his sentence. With precise movements he dialed his phone as he hurried inside the sod house. "Send someone to make an arrest," she heard him say. "A man has assaulted my daughter at the sod house. His name is Jeremy Parcet."

Jack wrapped Giselle in his arms. Alicia listened to the loving exchange between father and daughter. Moments later she followed them outside, to see Mr. Parcet's retreating figure.

"He's getting away," she said.

"So? Where's he going to go?" Jack asked, one eyebrow raised, a glint sparking in his blue eyes. "This is Churchill after all." He wrapped his arm around her waist. "You've got some explaining to do, Alicia." His gaze burrowed into her.

"Alicia protected me, Daddy." Giselle's voice grew stronger with every word. "She was like a mother bear protecting her cub. I never knew she could sound so fierce."

"I think there are a lot of things we don't know about Alicia." Jack squeezed Alicia's shoulder and whispered in her ear, "But I, for one, am eager to learn more."

"You won't like what you hear," she murmured. "It's not a pretty story."

"I don't care." He stopped, grasped both of her arms and faced her, eyes blazing with some emotion she didn't understand. "I'm not running from the tough parts anymore, Alicia. I've got God on my side. He'll help me face my fears and work through them. But I'm going to need your patience."

She didn't understand what had happened to him, but she knew this lighthearted attitude would disappear when he heard her story. Still, it was time to tell it.

"You and I need to talk," Jack said.

With a grim smile, Alicia agreed. It was time he knew the whole truth. Then her fairy-tale dream of being loved would be over. Once he knew the truth, Jack would want to get as far away from her as he could.

The sun was setting when Alicia and Jack finally left the medical center. Giselle was fine, but Jack had insisted she stay overnight just in case. Though Giselle protested, Tim Brown, the town's newest doctor, took one look at her daddy's fierce face and agreed she should stay.

Alicia would have left, but Jack insisted she stay with him to comfort Giselle as she repeated the afternoon's events over and over. Alicia marveled at the silent flow of mutual understanding she shared with Jack; they knew Giselle needed to talk out her feelings in order to deal with them. When the girl was finally worn out and her eyelids drooped, they still sat together, waiting for her to find the dreamless sleep that would heal her.

This, Alicia decided as they left the hospital, was what real parenting was about—being there for your kid. And she'd missed it all.

As if he understood her sadness, Jack's shoulder bumped hers as they walked toward the beach. He seemed to know she needed the sound of the waves over the graveled sand to bring some measure of peace to her heart. He chose a massive boulder, sat down and patted the space beside him. When she was seated he took her hand and held it.

"Tell me," he said, his eyes brimming with something Alicia had only ever dreamed of.

So she did. She told him about losing her parents, about moving to a city where she felt lost, alone and so vulnerable. She told him about the misery of not being able to understand and how no one seemed to care. She told him how hopeful she'd been the day she entered Mr. Parcet's remedial class and of how he'd paid her special attention.

"I thought he wanted to help me," she whispered, too ashamed to look at him. "I didn't understand that he wanted—" She couldn't say it.

"He raped you." She sensed he held himself in very tight control as he waited for her nod. "You didn't report him?"

"I didn't think anyone would listen to me," she whispered, staring at him, trying to make him understand. "He berated me so badly. By then I didn't know anything except that I couldn't go back to his class. I couldn't let it happen again. So I ran away." She bowed her head, stared at their joined hands. "I lived on the street. I was terrified I'd get caught or beaten up, or worse, but it was better than being near him, letting him…" She peeked at Jack, winced at his dark glower and couldn't continue.

"You did the right thing, Alicia." His voice came so gentle, so reassuring. His fingers tightened around hers. "Tell me all of it."

"I started getting sick." The fear rushed back, blocking her throat. She drew several calming breaths. "I heard about this place you could go and see a doctor. I met Nancy and Harold there."

"You were pregnant?"

"Yes." She gulped. "I was so scared. I didn't know what to do. I was only fifteen. I couldn't care for a baby." She let the tears fall, so tired of being strong. "Nancy and Harold took me in, loved me, cared for me. They taught me that God loved me, that I had a future."

"Tell me about your baby." Jack's quiet voice held reassurance but Alicia knew he'd soon change.

When he heard what she'd done, he'd look at her with loathing and disgust. But it had to be said. She had to tell him everything, even though it would cost her his respect.

"I gave him away," she blurted out. She had no way to stop the tears. They dripped down her face, onto their hands, a steady flow of misery, sadness and regret. "I knew I had to. He deserved a chance, a life and an opportunity to be the best he could be. I knew he wouldn't get that with me so I gave him away. I signed a paper saying I'd never look for him."

Jack didn't say anything.

"I gave my child away," she repeated, filled with shame. She tipped her face up, staring through the blur of tears at Jack's beloved face, trying to make him understand. "That's who I've been looking for. My son. I had to make sure he was safe, that Mr. Parcet—"

"Could never get his hands on him." Jack pulled her to his chest, his arms wrapping around her. "What courage you have, Alicia. Parcet is a powerful man to go against. He has money and, until recently, his father to get him out of scrapes." He smiled at her surprise. "My friends on the force keep me informed. I tried to get him twice for assaulting his coworkers but he slipped away both times. Yet you've managed to thwart his plans. He'll never inherit now."

To Alicia's utter astonishment, Jack Campbell

kissed her. Finally she came to enough to kiss him back, thrilled to the depths of her soul but mystified. When he drew away, she frowned at him.

"Aren't you shocked? Don't you hate what I did?" she whispered, unable to decipher the look on his dear face, the glow in his blue eyes.

"Why? Because you were such a strong mother that you'd rather give your child to someone so he could have a happy life than selfishly keep him?" he asked, shaking his head. "Because you did what you had to in order to keep that child away from a man who would have hurt him?" He cupped her face between her palms. "Because you were a loving mother?"

She nodded slowly as the spark of hope began to flicker inside. "All of those," she whispered.

"I'm proud," Jack told her, tracing her forehead, her eyes, her nose and finally her lips. "I am so proud to know you, Alicia Featherstone. You remind me of a polar bear— fiercely protective, doing whatever you have to in order to keep your precious cub safe, no matter what the danger."

The spark flickered and caught. Was that admiration she saw in his eyes?

"The thing is, we're all your cubs, aren't we?" He brushed her nose with his lips. "You fight for all of us, the Lives boys, Giselle, your people, the town. You'll take on anyone or anything. I love you, Alicia."

She couldn't believe it, and yet, there in the depths of those gorgeous blue eyes burned a truth she had to accept. Jack Campbell cared about *her*.

"But how? When?" she whispered, not quite ready to trust his words.

"When did I begin to love you?" He shook his head, his smile self-mocking. "I don't know. I guess you just grew on me from the first time we met. You're so incredible, so strong. I've never known anyone like you."

He leaned forward and kissed her until Alicia was breathless, but she knew there was something more he needed to say so she drew back and waited.

"I loved Simone. I grew up loving her. I never imagined anything but a future with her and when it ended, I decided I'd never love anyone again because losing hurt too much." He traced her cheekbones, then let his finger trail to her hair and the braids she wore. "I was determined. But then you came along. You became part of my life. But I was afraid. I needed to have control."

"What changed?" she whispered, loving his touch and the gentle smile that tipped his so-kissable lips.

"I was sitting in the church this afternoon and I heard you yell. And I thought, *What if I never get to tell her how much she means to me?* Losing someone you love hurts, Alicia, but never loving them would hurt so much more. I knew I'd never stop loving you." His mouth tightened. "Then I saw

Parcet and you said Giselle was injured and I knew I couldn't control the future. I couldn't control anything. All I could do was trust God with my future. And that's what I'm going to do."

"Just like that?"

He nodded, then tilted his head to one side and gave her a quizzical look. "Do you feel anything for me, Alicia?" he asked. The fear couched in those words was her undoing.

"I love you." He would have kissed her, but she held him back. She needed to say this. "I don't know anything about love, Jack. I'm not the kind of person you should love."

"What?" His nose wrinkled as it did when he was confused.

"I'm…used. I can't read and I had a baby. I—"

"Love you," he finished. "That's all you have to say. I love you. I don't care about anything else."

"You might one day," she worried. "People will talk when they find out."

"People will always talk. But you and I know the truth." Jack smiled when a frown furrowed her forehead. "You are a very precious child of the most high God. He loves every detail about you, that's why He made you this way. To Him you are great." He grinned. "Isn't that what you were preaching to Adam that day? 'Your Father made you perfect.' That's what I care about, not what others say."

Alicia stared into his face, bemused, afraid to

believe. Jack didn't care about her past, she realized. He truly didn't care, because he loved her. And she loved him.

He must have noticed something had changed, because he grasped her hands in his, knelt on the hard, cool rock and stared into her eyes. His voice brimmed with tenderness.

"Do you love me, Alicia? Will you marry me?"

"I love you very much, Jack. More than I ever imagined." She gave a yelp as he threw his arms around her. But then he kissed her and she could think of nothing to say for a very long time.

The sun had long since set by the time he took her home.

"We've talked about everything, my darling," Jack said, holding her, his chin resting on her head as they stood beneath the streetlamp. "But you never answered my question. Are you going to marry me?"

Alicia tilted her head back and stared into the face she'd never grow tired of.

"I don't know… You likened me to a polar bear," she chastised him, tongue in cheek. "Polar bears are huge."

"Polar bears are sleek, beautiful creatures. So strong, so powerful. Especially to the Cree," he said, eyes twinkling. "I would be honored to be married to a woman with the spirit of a polar bear."

She gave him a genuine smile. "I would be honored to be married to you, Jack Campbell," she whispered. "Honored and amazed and humbled and so, so happy." She kissed him, reveling in the burst of feelings she'd only ever dreamed about. "To think that God knew this would happen, even way back when we were both suffering."

"He's quite a God."

"He certainly is."

Epilogue

The wedding of Alicia Featherstone to Jack Campbell took place two days before Christmas. Alicia's friends rallied around her, helping her plan every detail. Perhaps that's why she felt so relaxed as Giselle and Laurel fussed over her white satin wedding dress.

"I wasn't going to wear white," she murmured. "I'm not sure—"

"Purity of heart is what matters," Laurel said. "Jack says you're the purest bride he's ever known."

"Do you think he'll like this?" Alicia smoothed a hand over the lovely fabric.

"Of course. But he loves you. And you love him. The dress is just a bonus." Laurel helped her put on her veil. "I've got to check on the boys. Are you okay with Giselle?"

"I'm fine with Giselle." She held out her hand and Giselle took it, her face beaming.

When they were alone, Giselle pulled an envelope out of her tiny handbag.

"You're going to be my mom, Alicia, and I couldn't be any happier. I love you. I think you and Daddy are going to be so happy."

"I think we are, too," Alicia said.

"This is my wedding present to you," Giselle whispered as she held out the envelope. "Please read it."

Alicia slid the paper out. Dear sweet Jack had found a teacher familiar with teaching people with dyslexia. Every night he helped her review the lessons and because of that Alicia was finally learning to read. Of course, she could only read a little so far, but she had years to learn. She studied the words carefully, hoping she wouldn't embarrass herself. Shock filled her. She read the paper twice, a third time, not because she couldn't understand, but because she was afraid to believe.

"It's from your son," Giselle whispered. "I wrote the adoption agency and told them your story. I begged them to give you some information so you could stop worrying about him." She gulped, brushed away a tear. "His name is James. He has two brothers and one sister and he's very happy in his home."

"He says they taught him about his heritage and he's very proud to be part Cree." Tears rolled down Alicia's face. "He thanks me for loving him enough to give him a family."

"The adoption agency said he told them that you're welcome to visit him anytime," Giselle said, her face glowing. "He wants to meet his mom."

"Oh, Giselle, thank you. I've never had such a lovely gift." They were still hugging and crying when Laurel returned.

"Jack wants to know what's taking so long," she said as she helped Alicia repair her makeup. "He's afraid you're backing out."

"No way." Alicia smoothed her dress, took her bouquet from Giselle and grinned. "Let's get me married!"

She moved to the back of the church, her gaze drawn to the tall, commanding and very dear man whose face transformed when he caught sight of her. Jack grinned as Laurel led the way down the aisle. He smiled at his daughter when she followed, but his attention remained focused on Alicia from her first step until she was standing by his side.

"Like I said," he whispered. "Beautiful as a polar bear."

Alicia couldn't suppress her chuckle. Then Rick began to speak—beautiful, moving words about God's plan for love and the bonds it forged. Jack's fingers curled around Alicia's when the Lives' boys led the kids' choir in an Aboriginal song about the Creator and His love. Then she and Jack said their vows.

"My darling Alicia, this is the first step of our walk together with God. I will always love you, always be there for you, support you and want the best for you. Together we will seek and do His will. You are my heart."

Alicia accepted the plain gold ring on her finger, overwhelmed by the love she saw in his eyes, love for her. She tipped her face up.

"Jack, I thank God daily for sending you into my life. You are everything I dared to dream of. I am the most blessed of women because of your love." She slid his ring in place, holding his gaze, letting her eyes say what she could not find words for. Vaguely she heard Rick pronounce them man and wife.

Jack's eyes flared as Rick said, "You may kiss your bride."

"I love you, Alicia," he whispered, his lips inches from her.

"I love you," she whispered back.

As they kissed it seemed to Alicia that the entire community of Churchill applauded.

"I love you, Daddy," Giselle said, flinging her arms around them. "And Mom."

Alicia hugged her back, but she couldn't say anything. Her heart was too full. She was finally going to be a mom. God had given her a family. She belonged.

* * * * *

Dear Reader,

Welcome back!

I hope you've enjoyed Alicia and Jack's story. Each of them had to work through their faith in different ways, but both realized that God does answer prayer, even if it's not when or in the way we expect.

I hope you'll check in again soon for the fourth story in my Northern Lights series, coming in late 2014. You know there's always something happening in polar bear country.

Till then I wish you magnificent dreams that come true when you awaken. I wish that you may laugh heartily, cry openly, sing loudly, dance wildly and love unashamedly. I wish you may feel grateful at all times, especially when life is not comfortable. I wish you may realize what an incredible being you are. Most of all I wish that you will grow in our Father's abundant love and grace.

Blessings,

Lois Richer

Questions for Discussion

1. If you had been able to advise Alicia after she had been raped, what advice would you have given—adopt or keep the baby? Discuss why you made your choice.

2. Giselle was also adopted and it was kept secret from her. Given what you've learned about her past, would you, as her adoptive mother, also make this choice? What would make you reconsider?

3. The loss of his wife left Jack reeling, afraid God would take away more in his life if he didn't control things. Can you think of times in your own life when you felt keeping control would help? Did it?

4. Alicia's difficulty reading caused many problems in her life. Discuss ways parents, teachers and community members can help catch kids in need and ensure problem areas are addressed.

5. Alicia felt that her parents did not prepare her for the racial bias she later encountered. Do you agree? How might you have handled such a sensitive issue?

6. Racial prejudice thrives all over the world. Discuss ways we can teach our children to respect the uniqueness of every culture, even though we might disagree with some of their practices.

7. At first Jack didn't want to be involved with the sod house project, but then he realized he enjoyed working with others on it. What changed? Consider how our wrong expectations may color our perceptions. How does one become more open-minded?

8. Did you feel empathetic toward Giselle's situation? How do you feel adoptions should be handled? Suggest alternative ways to give the adopted child more control over their future.

9. Churchill is a small, isolated, multicultural community. Many people go there for its wilderness setting. Do you think this is a good location for the Lives Under Construction facility? Why?

10. Discuss options one may use to protect children from a "Mr. Parcet" in their communities, schools and churches. Do you feel Alicia was wrong not to report him?

11. Jack worried Giselle might not fit in in Churchill. In this age of increased mobility, are there ways

to help ease a child's move to a new school and community? Provide a list of resources the child can use to feel more comfortable.

12. Do you know someone who has been adopted and is unable to locate their birth parents? How can you help?

LARGER-PRINT BOOKS!

GET 2 FREE
LARGER-PRINT NOVELS
PLUS 2 FREE
MYSTERY GIFTS

Love Inspired®

SUSPENSE
RIVETING INSPIRATIONAL ROMANCE

Larger-print novels are now available...

YES! Please send me 2 FREE LARGER-PRINT Love Inspired® Suspense novels and my 2 FREE mystery gifts (gifts are worth about $10). After receiving them, if I don't wish to receive any more books, I can return the shipping statement marked "cancel." If I don't cancel, I will receive 4 brand-new novels every month and be billed just $5.24 per book in the U.S. or $5.74 per book in Canada. That's a savings of at least 23% off the cover price. It's quite a bargain! Shipping and handling is just 50¢ per book in the U.S. and 75¢ per book in Canada.* I understand that accepting the 2 free books and gifts places me under no obligation to buy anything. I can always return a shipment and cancel at any time. Even if I never buy another book, the two free books and gifts are mine to keep forever.

110/310 IDN F5CC

Name	(PLEASE PRINT)	

Address		Apt. #

City	State/Prov.	Zip/Postal Code

Signature (if under 18, a parent or guardian must sign)

Mail to the Harlequin® Reader Service:
IN U.S.A.: P.O. Box 1867, Buffalo, NY 14240-1867
IN CANADA: P.O. Box 609, Fort Erie, Ontario L2A 5X3

**Are you a current subscriber to Love Inspired Suspense books
and want to receive the larger-print edition?
Call 1-800-873-8635 or visit www.ReaderService.com.**

* Terms and prices subject to change without notice. Prices do not include applicable taxes. Sales tax applicable in N.Y. Canadian residents will be charged applicable taxes. Offer not valid in Quebec. This offer is limited to one order per household. Not valid for current subscribers to Love Inspired Suspense larger-print books. All orders subject to credit approval. Credit or debit balances in a customer's account(s) may be offset by any other outstanding balance owed by or to the customer. Please allow 4 to 6 weeks for delivery. Offer available while quantities last.

Your Privacy—The Harlequin® Reader Service is committed to protecting your privacy. Our Privacy Policy is available online at www.ReaderService.com or upon request from the Harlequin Reader Service.

We make a portion of our mailing list available to reputable third parties that offer products we believe may interest you. If you prefer that we not exchange your name with third parties, or if you wish to clarify or modify your communication preferences, please visit us at www.ReaderService.com/consumerschoice or write to us at Harlequin Reader Service Preference Service, P.O. Box 9062, Buffalo, NY 14269. Include your complete name and address.

LISLPDIR13R